OSPREY GAMES
Bloomsbury Publishing Plc
Kemp House, Chawley Park, Cumnor Hill, Oxford OX2 9PH, UK
29 Earlsfort Terrace, Dublin 2, Ireland
1385 Broadway, 5th Floor, New York, NY 10018, USA
E-mail: info@ospreygames.co.uk
www.ospreygames.co.uk

OSPREY GAMES is a trademark of Osprey Publishing Ltd

First published in Great Britain in 2021

A catalogue record for this book is available from the British Library.

ISBN: HB 9781472837509; eBook 9781472837516; ePDF 9781472837486; XML 9781472837493

21 22 23 24 25   10 9 8 7 6 5 4 3 2 1

Originated by PDQ Digital Media Solutions, Bungay, UK
Printed and bound in India by Replika Press Private Ltd.

Osprey Games supports the Woodland Trust, the UK's leading woodland conservation charity.

To find out more about our authors and books visit www.ospreypublishing.com. Here you will find
extracts, author interviews, details of forthcoming events and the option to sign up for our newsletter.

CONTENTS

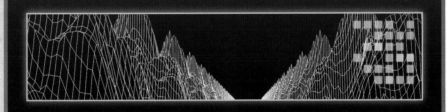

INCOMING TRANSMISSION

In a galaxy torn apart by the Last War, vast pirate fleets roam from system to system, robbing, extorting, and rounding up slaves. Any attempt to form any kind of central authority larger than a city state is quickly and brutally crushed. In this dark time, the only way to survive is to stay small and inconspicuous. Amidst this chaos, however, thousands of independent crews manage to carry on their business. Smugglers, relic hunters, freedom fighters, and mercenaries roam the dead stars in small ships, scratching out a living anyway they can…

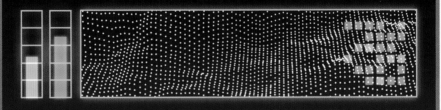

INTRODUCTION

Welcome to *Stargrave*, a narrative wargame in which the players assemble a small crew of science-fiction adventurers, and then chart their story as they try to survive in the Ravaged Galaxy. Just by playing through the scenarios in this book, the crews will explore an abandoned research station, battle strange creatures in a dense swamp, scavenge weapons from a derelict warship, and shoot it out with gangs in a sewer-system. All of this while trying to stay one step ahead of the brutal pirate fleets.

In this book you will find all of the information you need to play the game, including rules for how to create your captain and their crew, how to set up a table, and how to fight for possession of valuable loot! While these rules might look intimidating at first, especially if you have never played a wargame before, they are generally straightforward, and most people will have a pretty firm grasp of most of the rules after playing just a few turns.

Games of *Stargrave* are generally quick, and once you have learned the rules you should have no problem completing a game in a couple of hours. Although one-off games can be fun, it is by combining all of your games into an ongoing campaign that you will get the most out of *Stargrave*. By playing through a campaign, your crew will grow in power and experience. And you can spend the loot you acquire during games to expand your crew, buy advanced technology weapons and equipment, and even upgrade your starship.

While *Stargrave* is designed to be a competitive game between two or more players, it is less concerned with being a tactical exercise and more interested in helping players achieve a shared sense of fun and adventure as their crews explore the dark, dangerous, and potentially profitable corners of a galaxy that has been ripped apart by war. These rules attempt to cover all of the situations that are likely to occur during play but, without a doubt, there will be times when the exact rule for a given situation is unclear. In these cases, the first question to ask is: 'What would happen in the movie?' Or, to put it another way, decide on the coolest, most dramatic, cinematic result and go with that. This is a game about high drama, big moments, and big explosions!

Always remember, these rules have been created for one purpose: for players to have fun. If there is any aspect of the game you want to change, any rules you want to add, or any ideas you want to incorporate that will make the game more fun for you and your gaming buddies, then please do so! Having fun is the point of playing a game, after all.

Finally, one of the best parts of wargaming is that it is a social activity. Even at home, players like to go online to talk about their games, discuss rules, show off their models and terrain, and just chat with people who have similar interests. Be sure to check out the *Stargrave: Science-Fiction Wargames in the Ravaged Galaxy* Facebook group, as well as places such as Board Game Geek, Reddit, and the Lead Adventure Forum. Also, to get all of the latest news and updates, take a look at my blog: **therenaissancetroll.blogspot.co.uk.**

WHAT YOU WILL NEED TO PLAY

To play *Stargrave* you will need several things besides this book: a table, miniature figures, a tape measure or ruler marked in inches ("), a couple of twenty-sided dice (d20s), a copy of the Crew Sheet from the back of the book, and a pencil. Ideally, you will also have a selection of terrain pieces that you can use to set up a tactically interesting table. If you are new to the world of tabletop wargaming, some of these items might not be immediately obvious and are explained below.

MINIATURES

Miniatures (or figures, or models) are the focus of the tabletop wargaming hobby, and the main reason that most of us entered into it. Essentially, they are toy soldiers made out of metal, resin or plastic, often sculpted to an extremely high level of detail. Official *Stargrave* miniatures are available from North Star Military Figures (www.northstarfigures.com) as well as many other dealers, and provide options for all of the different captains and crewmen in the game, as well as many of the alien creatures that might be encountered. It is not mandatory to use 'official miniatures' to play the game, though. There are loads of really cool science fiction miniatures on the market, representing all the facets and sub-genres of sci-fi, and players should see this game as an opportunity to pick up the ones they've always wanted, but never previously had a use for. It is worth mentioning that most miniatures are supplied unpainted, and many wargamers find that painting miniatures is their favourite part of the hobby.

Stargrave was designed for use with 28mm miniatures, which is the most common and popular size. Larger and smaller miniatures are also available, and it is perfectly acceptable to use those instead, provided all of the players are using the same size! Players using larger or smaller miniatures may want to adjust some of the distances for movement and weapon ranges to get the correct 'feel', but otherwise, size makes little difference.

Players should do their best to obtain miniatures that match the characters they are designed to represent, with appropriate weapons and armour. However, this is not always possible, and as long as it is clear to all of the players which figures represent which characters, the exact appearance is not important. In fact, even the race of the character is not important. The *Stargrave* universe includes numerous alien species. Most of these are humanoid, but not all. If you want to make up a crew of spacefaring wolfmen, or human-sized insects, or even large amoeboids, go for it.

Most wargamers mount their miniatures on bases. These are typically metal or plastic disks between 25 and 32mm in diameter. In *Stargrave*, the size of a figure's base makes very little difference, and players should feel free to use whatever base size they find most visually appealing for their miniatures.

Stargrave also uses a couple of varieties of loot tokens. While these can be anything from coins to bits of shiny paper, players will need to mark which ones are which type – so they may want to get specific ones to represent the different types of loot. This is explained in greater detail later in the rules.

DICE

Many of the actions your figures will attempt in *Stargrave*, such as using special powers or fighting, require the player to roll a die in order to determine success or failure. *Stargrave* uses a twenty-sided die (often just referred to as a d20) for all rolls. Each player will need one d20 to play. While d20s are rarely seen in most traditional board games, they are used in a lot of speciality games and are obtainable from most game stores or online.

THE TABLE

Once you have your miniatures and dice ready to go, you are going to need a table to play on. Games of *Stargrave* are normally played on square tables with sides about 3 feet long. In games with more than two players, you may want to consider increasing the table size, up to 4' x 4', to give everyone more room to manoeuvre. If large tables are hard to come by, as they are in my house, you can play games of *Stargrave* on smaller tables. 2' x 2' is probably the minimum you will need to play a game. Smaller tables tend to make for quicker, bloodier games, but that doesn't mean they are less fun!

TERRAIN

The universe of *Stargrave* is vast and includes thousands of different planets. When setting up a table, players are limited only by their imaginations. Games can be set in run-down starports, asteroid mining complexes, steaming jungles, crowded cities, desert canyons, or any other cool setting.

The key when setting up a table for *Stargrave* is that it is crowded with terrain. If a crew wants to survive, it is essential that they stick to the shadows. If they come out into the open, they'll quickly be wiped out by one of the large pirate fleets. So, when setting up, make sure to give them plenty of cover to hide behind! Besides, the more terrain, the more fun that games tend to be!

Now, it would be great if everyone owned enough terrain to set up tables for numerous different settings, but that is, of course, not the case. If most of your terrain is urban – that's fine – your crew obviously likes working in urban environments. If you mainly have forests, maybe your crew specializes in wilderness operations. If you are just starting out in the hobby, you may not have any of this – that's fine too. In that case, you might consider buying a cheap set of blocks. These blocks can then be used to create all kinds of different table set-ups. You can even spray-paint them a steel grey if you want, so that they look like the walls of a spaceship or the sides of buildings. Don't worry, once you are playing the game your imagination will 'fill in the gaps' and turn any set-up into a dangerous shanty town or robotic factory.

So long as there is a lot of 'stuff' on the table for figures to hide behind, clamber over, and fight upon, the specific look of the terrain is not important.

THE CREW SHEET AND TEMPLATES

At the back of the book (see page 162) you will find a copy of the Crew Sheet, which is used to keep track of your captain and their crew. Each player will need a copy of this sheet. You can either photocopy the sheet from the back of the book, or you can download a copy from the Osprey Games website (www.ospreygames.co.uk). At the same time, you can copy or download the templates that are used to determine the area of effect for flamethrowers and grenades.

CHAPTER ONE
ASSEMBLING A CREW

The galaxy is a rough place. Most of the once-powerful planets have been reduced to rubble, their populations decimated. Even the smaller colonies that were left untouched by the war have seen their economies collapse as necessary trade dried up. Vast pirate fleets roam between the stars, taking what they want and enforcing their own brand of law and justice. Plagues have run unchecked through many systems. Famine has turned others into wastelands. Raiding, border skirmishes, and other low-level warfare is rife.

It is against this background that the 'independent crews' operate. Generally consisting of a single ship and a small crew, these small bands travel between the systems, keeping to the shadows and out-of-sight of the pirate fleets. Some crews are freedom-fighters looking to strike against the pirates or idealists looking to rebuild civilization. Others are treasure hunters, picking through the ruins for lost technology and other valuable artefacts. Still others are bounty hunters, religious crusaders, shady merchants, pirates, or criminals on the run. In truth, there are as many causes and reasons to fly between the stars as there are spaceships.

The first step in creating your independent crew is sketching out a mental picture of the crew you want to play. Is your crew the remnants of a military unit, still desperately trying to fight the Last War? A group of nearly extinct aliens desperately seeking other survivors of their race? Or a team of art experts who 'recover' lost artworks from ruined planets in the hope of selling them for a premium to collectors amongst the pirates? While these decisions have no specific impact on your crew in terms of rules, having a few broad outlines in mind will help with the rest of the process and give you a starting point in telling the story of your crew.

Once you've got your basic idea, it is time to create your captain.

CREATING A CAPTAIN

Every independent crew is led by a **Captain**. This is not necessarily a military rank, but simply denotes that the person commands a starship, even a small one. In game terms, the captain is your most important figure. The captain is both the leader of your independent crew and your most powerful figure. Essentially, the captain represents you on the tabletop.

To create a captain, you'll want to have a copy of the Crew Sheet from the back of the book (see page 162). The sheet has space for all of the important information about your captain (and their crew) that you will need during a game.

The first decision you should make when creating a captain is their name and species. Neither of these decisions will affect the character's in-game capabilities, but they will help establish them in your mind. Some people like to find a miniature they really love and tell a story around it. Others go the opposite direction and create a character first, then find a figure to fit. Either way is fine.

In a galaxy consisting of tens of thousands of worlds, each with a unique culture, almost any name you can think of will be appropriate – so you might as well go with something that sounds cool to you. Of course, when thinking up a name, it might help to know your captain's species. There are nearly as many species in the galaxy as there are planets. Most of these are humanoid, but some are decidedly not. Feel free to have your captain be of any species, as long as that species is generally human-sized, but realize that, gamewise, any difference between that species and humans is purely cosmetic (for more information on alien species in *Stargrave*, see the text box on page 27).

BACKGROUND

Once you've established a mental picture of your captain, it is time to select your captain's background. There are eight different backgrounds open to captains, each with its own strengths and weaknesses. When choosing a background, it is best to study the capabilities of each and decide which fits best with your play style. If you like charging in and taking the fight to the enemy, you might consider a Biomorph. If you like to work from the back, manipulating people and objects, a Psionicist might be more your style.

Listed below are the backgrounds open to captains, along with a brief description of their abilities, their typical look, and their most common motivations for the adventuring life. Of course, all of these are generalizations, and it is fine to have a captain who is an outlier for their background.

Below each description is a list of stat modifications and core powers for that background. This is explained in the next section.

Biomorph

When the old empires fell, so did their laws limiting 'genetic enhancement'. A few scientists seized this opportunity to engage in radical experimentation. This involved both the genetic manipulation of naturally born individuals and the creation of wholly new 'tank-born' individuals. In either case, those that survived these experiments often had unique abilities to control their own bodies, such as realigning their skeletal structure, growing new limbs, changing their skin tones, or even growing additional organs to deal with toxic substances or alien environments. Unfortunately, many biomorphs were also left psychically scarred by their modifications. While the worst of these tend to destroy themselves quickly, almost all carry some form of phobia, psychosis, or other mental impairment.

Depending on the abilities of a biomorph, they tend to dress in loose, or very stretchy outfits, or have specialized suits of armour made that take into account their abilities. More than any other background, biomorphs tend to form independent crews because they are on the run – either from those that created them or want to do further experiments on them, or to escape the consequences of some crime (often unintended).

BIOMORPH	
STAT MODIFICATIONS	+1 Health and choose two of the following: +1 Move, +1 Fight, +1 Shoot
CORE POWERS	Adrenaline Surge, Armour Plates, Camouflage, Fling, Regenerate, Restructure Body, Toxic Claws, Toxic Secretion

Cyborg

A fusion of man and machine, cyborgs have been a constant, if rare, feature of every war for the past several centuries. Specialist cyborgs have been created to fulfil nearly every military role including infiltration, stealth, reconnaissance, or just straight-up combat. Despite their obvious advantages, cyborgs are rarely cost effective and thus were never produced in great numbers.

With the end of the Last War, many cyborgs attempted to 'retire', but most found that it requires huge sums of money to keep their bodies working. For that reason, many have gone into business for themselves, working as mercenaries, bounty hunters, private investigators, or retrieval specialists.

Cyborgs vary greatly in appearance. Some are indistinguishable from humans, some look like humans with obvious robotic parts, and a few look completely robotic and only feature a human brain or nervous system.

CYBORG	
STAT MODIFICATIONS	+1 Health and choose two of the following: +1 Move, +1 Fight, +1 Shoot
CORE POWERS	Camouflage, Control Robot, Data Knock, Energy Shield, Power Spike, Quick Step, Target Lock, Temporary Upgrade

Mystic

As the galaxy exploded during the Last War, many people turned to religion to try to find solace. The first, and most obvious, expression of this was the doomsday cults. Some of these grew out of ancient orders that could trace their origins back for millennia; others seemed to spontaneously germinate from the apocalyptic death-tolls. Most of these cults were quickly exterminated or destroyed themselves, but a few survived and even thrived. By mixing mysticism, alien technology, and 'dark science', these surviving cults developed strange and deadly powers. While not all of them are 'evil', most people look upon these cultists as witches and warlocks and they are rarely welcome. These cult mystics tend to travel between the stars searching for various things: ancient mystical texts, alien technology, or new secrets of dark science.

There was also a quieter reaction to the war, the flourishing of monastic orders. While these orders have wildly differing foci, from healing to research, historical preservation, even military prowess, they all believe in the establishment and maintenance of order. It is not unusual for a monastery to take the surrounding towns and villages under their protection, and because of this, these areas have often become havens in this dark time.

In order to join one of these orders, an aspirant must demonstrate a deep connectedness to the universe around them. It is unknown if this is the result of some physiological attribute or simply an open-mindedness to the possibilities beyond sight. Either way, it has allowed these mystics to develop abilities that seem to go beyond the normal bounds of physics.

Whether a cultist, monk, or even knight, these mystics generally wear loose, non-descript clothing, often robes. While armour is worn by a few of the more military focused monastic orders, it seems to interfere with the abilities of most mystics.

MYSTIC	
STAT MODIFICATIONS	+2 Will, + 1 Health, and choose one of the following: +1 Move, +1 Fight, +1 Shoot
CORE POWERS	Control Animal, Dark Energy, Heal, Life Leach, Mystic Trance, Puppet Master, Suggestion, Void Blade

Robotics Expert

Few people truly understand robots. Even those who build and repair them rarely grasp the nuances of how they think and what motivates them beyond their basic programming. The exceptions are known as Robotics Experts. These people, who are often socially awkward with their own kind, seem to share an empathy, or a fluency, with these constructs.

Robotics Experts are generally master craftsmen, building the best, most capable, and most intelligent robots. Not only that, but they are able to network these robots together in ways that other people can't even begin to understand. It is not unusual for a robotics expert captain to have more robots than people in their crew, and such crews tend to operate together with a high degree of efficiency.

Robotics Experts are always looking for new technology, and more funds, to improve their robots and push the bounds of what is possible. This leads many to become mercenaries and smugglers. Robotics Experts tend to focus on their work and are unconcerned with their appearance. They generally carry a lot of tools and spare parts for their 'children'.

ROBOTICS EXPERT	
STAT MODIFICATIONS	+1 Will and choose two of the following: +1 Move, +1 Fight, +1 Shoot, +1 Health
CORE POWERS	Control Robot, Create Robot, Drone, Electromagnetic Pulse, Remote Firing, Remote Guidance, Repair Robot, Re-wire Robot

Rogue

While law and order has broken down across most of the galaxy, rogues never paid it much attention anyway. Their only law was the law of not getting caught. This background includes such shifty characters as smugglers, gamblers, fixers, shady merchants, drug dealers, etc.

Rogues have learned to survive the horrors of the galaxy through a combination of wit, brains, and luck. While they generally don't have any mystical powers or bodily enhancements, they know when to press their luck and when to scarper when a deal goes sour. While rogues rarely appear like the most dangerous of individuals, they almost always have several back-up plans, a lucky coin in their pocket, and a powerful firearm concealed up their sleeve.

Rogues travel between the stars always searching for the deal that will make them rich.

ROGUE	
STAT MODIFICATIONS	+1 Will, +1 Health, and choose two of the following: +1 Move, +1 Fight, +1 Shoot
CORE POWERS	Bait and Switch, Bribe, Cancel Power, Concealed Firearm, Data Jump, Fortune, Haggle, Quick-Step

Psionicist

Over the last few centuries, psionics – the ability to shape and affect reality with nothing more than the mind – has become an accepted, if extremely rare, branch of science. While most of the institutions and schools set up to promote, train, and study psionically gifted individuals were deliberately targeted and destroyed in the Last War, many of the students survived.

Psionicists vary wildly in their abilities. Some can move objects or conjure fire, while others can enter people's minds and potentially control their bodies. Because of their rare abilities, psionicists are actively recruited by the pirate fleets, and those that will not join up willingly are often kidnapped. Thus, the life of a psionicist is inherently dangerous, leading many to live a life on the run, forming their own independent crews to fight against, or at least stay one step ahead of, the pirate fleets.

Psionicists tend to keep a low-profile and thus wear 'normal clothes'. That said, many shave their heads as their hair becomes itchy when using their powers. Many also feel compelled to sketch very specific, unique tattoos on their bodies, though the reasons for this have never been understood. Psionicists rarely wear armour as it can impair their abilities.

PSIONICIST	
STAT MODIFICATIONS	+2 Will, +1 Health and choose one of the following: +1 Move, +1 Fight, +1 Shoot
CORE POWERS	Break Lock, Destroy Weapon, Lift, Psionic Fire, Psychic Shield, Pull, Suggestion, Wall of Force

Tekker

Considering the size of the galaxy, it is inevitable that technology advances much faster in some corners than in others. Even with modern star travel, the spread of such technology can be slow. When the Last War destroyed most of the great civilizations of the galaxy, the average level of technology in the galaxy dropped precipitately, essentially creating a dark age in most places.

Although the means to construct most of the highest-level technology was destroyed, many examples of those technologies still exist, and a few people still have the skills to repair it. Such individuals earn a reputation as 'Tekkers', as they always seem to be fiddling with some strange and wonderful device.

While Tekkers run the gamut in terms of appearance, they all tend to carry lots of high-tech equipment and individualized tool kits.

TEKKER	
STAT MODIFICATIONS	+2 Will and choose two of the following: +1 Move, +1 Fight, +1 Shoot, +1 Health
CORE POWERS	Anti-gravity Projection, Data Jump, Data Knock, Data Skip, Drone, Electromagnetic Pulse, Holographic Wall, Transport

Veteran

The Last War saw more people take up arms than at any point in the history of the galaxy. While trillions lost their lives in the countless horrific battles, many survived to see the desolate aftermath. When the central governments of the two great empires collapsed, most of these veterans were left to their own devices. Most attempted to return home and pick up the pieces of their old lives, but many found their homes destroyed and their loved ones gone. Others knew that war had changed them so badly that they could never go home again.

In the early days after the war, it was not uncommon for veterans to band together into small armies, but most of these were wiped out by the pirate fleets. Most of the veterans that survived did so by hiding, or forming their own, small, independent crews that could move around without drawing too much attention.

Many veterans continue to fight for some lost cause: their empire, their planet, or just a sense of justice. Others have abandoned any hope of a sane galaxy and have become mercenaries, bounty-hunters, and raiders. Some are just looking for a way to use the skills they have to feed their families.

Veterans have been trained to fight and have come to realize that their survival depends on a combination of skill, luck, and good equipment. Veterans always wear the best armour and carry the best weapons they can find.

VETERAN	
STAT MODIFICATIONS	+1 Fight, +1 Health, and choose one of the following: +1 Move, +1 Fight (for a total of +2), +1 Shoot
CORE POWERS	Armoury, Command, Coordinated Fire, Energy Shield, Fortune, Power Spike, Remote Firing, Target Designation

CHOOSING POWERS

Now that your captain has a background, you must choose their starting powers. These are the special abilities that make your captain unique, and selecting them is one of the most important decisions you will make. These powers give your crew special advantages that you can hopefully use to help defeat your enemies.

Under the description of each of the backgrounds is a list of **Core Powers** for that background. Each of these powers is explained fully in Chapter Four: Powers (see pages 105–116). A starting captain gets to choose five powers. The player must choose either three or four (their choice) of these powers from the core powers for the captain's background. The other one or two must be selected from any of the powers listed in Chapter Four, so long as they are not among your core powers.

When selecting a power, write that power on the crew sheet in the appropriate space under the captain. Next to each space for writing a power is a space to write the power's activation number. The lower the activation number, the easier it is for the captain to use this power during the game. If this is one of the core powers for your captain's background, the activation number is equal to the one listed for that power. If this power is not one of your core powers, then the activation number is equal to the one listed for that power +2. This means that powers from outside of a captain's core powers are harder to use.

Once this is done, you may decrease the activation number for two different powers by 1 each, regardless of whether or not these powers are core powers.

Each of the power slots on the captain sheet also includes a column for Strain. The Strain for each power is listed in its description. This number is fixed; it doesn't matter if the power is a Core Power or not.

As a captain participates in a campaign, they will gain new powers, and become better skilled at using the powers they have. This is explained in Chapter Three: Campaigns (see page 74).

THE STAT-LINE

In *Stargrave*, every figure – be it a captain, soldier, or alien creature – has a **Stat-line**, which determines its effectiveness in the game. There are six stats, explained below.

- **Move (M):** the speed of a figure. The higher its Move, the further it can move each turn.
- **Fight (F):** the figure's skill in hand-to-hand combat, and its ability to avoid incoming fire.
- **Shoot (S):** the figure's skill with projectile weapons.
- **Armour (A):** how much physical protection a figure is wearing, including armour and energy shielding.
- **Will (W):** the figure's determination, courage, and ability to work with technology.
- **Health (H):** the physical toughness of a figure and how much Damage it can endure before it is badly wounded or killed.

Each stat has a number associated with it. Put simply, the higher the number, the better. The specific meaning of each number will be explained later. For now, it is only important to know that every captain starts with the same base stat line listed below.

STARTING CAPTAIN					
M	F	S	A	W	H
6	+3	+2	9	+3	16

Stat Modifications

Before writing your captain's stats on the Crew Sheet, refer back to the description of their background. Each background has specific 'stat modifications' listed in the table beneath its description. Some of these modifiers are fixed, and others are offered as a choice. Apply all of these stat modifications to the starting captain's base stat line, as seen above, and write them in the appropriate section on the Crew Sheet.

Split Stats

In some circumstances, it will be necessary to record two different values for one stat. This is called a **Split Stat** and will be indicated as '+2/+3'. In these cases, the first number is always the figures' **actual stat**, and the second number is its **effective stat** in the current circumstances. Split stats usually occur when a figure is using some form of advanced technology, is under the effects of a power, or suffering from some form of injury. All of these instances will be fully explained later.

LEVEL

All Captains start at Level 15. This is explained in Chapter Three: Campaigns (see page 75).

GEAR

Captains have six slots for carrying gear. A starting captain may choose their gear from the General Equipment List (see page 29). There is no cost for this gear beyond the number of slots they take up. During a campaign, captains are allowed to change their gear after each game, so if they find an advanced carbine, a weird bit of alien technology, or cache of grenades, they can carry them in their next game. Alternatively, they can take different items from the General Equipment List after each game.

And that's essentially it for creating a captain; they are ready to go. That said, loners don't last long on the rough edge of the galaxy. In the next section, you will learn how to assemble a crew of followers to join your captain on its missions and explorations.

CREATING A FIRST MATE

Also called first officers, XOs, lieutenants, and occasionally 'Number 1', the **First Mate** is the captain's right-hand being. It is the first mate's job to oversee the day-to-day running of the crew while the captain deals with higher-level plans.

Every crew features a first mate, and creating one follows the same system as creating a captain. First you must pick a background for the first mate. This can be the same background as the captain, but does not have to be. It is perfectly acceptable to have a Tekker captain and a Cyborg first mate, or the other way around.

Next, choose the first mate's powers. First mates have four starting powers: two or three (player's choice) must be selected from the core powers, the remainder must be selected from any listed in the Chapter Four: Powers, so long as they are not core powers. When assigning activation numbers for each power, take the activation number listed for that power and add +2 if it is a core power, +4 if it is not. Thus, not only do first mates have fewer starting powers, but they aren't quite as good at using the ones they do have. That's why they are first mates and not captains!

FIRST MATE STATS

First mates have the following base stat-line. Like captains, first mates should apply the stat modifiers from their background to get their starting stats.

STARTING FIRST MATE					
M	F	S	A	W	H
6	+2	+2	9	+2	14

FIRST MATE LEVEL

All first mates start out at level 0. This is explained in the Chapter Three: Campaigns (see page 75).

FIRST MATE GEAR

First mates have five gear slots. They may choose starting gear from the General Equipment List in the same way as the captain.

RECRUITING SOLDIERS

Now that you've got your commanders in place, it is time to fill out the rest of your crew. For the sake of simplicity, all of the members of the crew who are not a captain or first mate are called soldiers. They may not actually be 'soldiers' by background, but in the tough world of the independent crews, everyone is called upon to fight sooner or later.

Every captain starts with 400 credits (cr) which can be used to recruit up to 8 soldiers to join their crew, of which a maximum of 4 can be specialists. To recruit a soldier, the captain simply pays the cost given on the tables below. This represents a combination of the cost of the soldier's gear, upkeep, pay etc. In most cases, the soldier actually follows their captain out of loyalty.

A few soldiers are 'free', meaning that no payment is necessary to recruit them. In this way, a captain should always be able field a full complement of 8 soldiers, even if funds are running a bit low!

Each soldier has fixed stats listed on the charts below. Unlike captains and first mates, the stats of a soldier are never modified, unless they are subject to some outside affect like advanced technology or a power. The Crew Sheet contains space to list all of your soldiers and their stats. You can give them all names if you wish, but in the rough galaxy of *Stargrave*, it is best not to get too attached them…

All Soldiers are equipped with the gear listed in their profile. In addition, they have 1 gear slot.

The stats given for each soldier incorporates any bonuses or penalties to their Move or Armour Stats provided by the items listed in their notes.

STANDARD SOLDIER TABLE

SOLDIER	MOVE	FIGHT	SHOOT	ARMOUR	WILL	HEALTH	COST	NOTES
Recruit	6	+2	+2	10	+0	12	Free	Pistol, Light Armour, Knife
Runner	7	+2	+1	9	+1	12	Free	Pistol, Knife
Hacker	6	+1	+1	10	+1	12	20cr	Pistol, Deck, Light Armour, Knife
Chiseler	6	+1	+1	10	+1	12	20cr	Pistol, Picks, Light Armour, Knife
Guard Dog	8	+1	+0	8	-2	10	10cr	Animal, Cannot carry gear or loot.
Sentry	5	+3	+2	11	+0	14	50cr	Carbine, Heavy Armour, Hand Weapon
Trooper	5	+2	+3	11	+0	14	50cr	Carbine, Heavy Armour, Knife
Medic	7	+2	+2	10	+3	14	100cr	Pistol, Light Armour, Medic Kit

SPECIALIST SOLDIER TABLE

SOLDIER	MOVE	FIGHT	SHOOT	ARMOUR	WILL	HEALTH	COST	NOTES
Codebreaker	6	+3	+2	10	+2	14	75cr	Carbine, Deck, Light Armour, Knife
Casecracker	6	+3	+2	10	+2	14	75cr	Carbine, Picks, Light Armour, Knife
Commando	5	+3	+3	11	+1	14	75cr	Carbine, Grenades*, Heavy Armour, Hand Weapon
Pathfinder	7	+3	+3	10	+2	14	100cr	Carbine, Grenades*, Light Armour, Hand Weapon
Sniper	6	+3	+4	10	+3	14	100cr	Carbine, Light Armour, Hand Weapon
Grenadier	5	+3	+3	11	+2	14	100cr	Grenade Launcher*, Pistol, Heavy Armour, Knife
Burner	5	+3	+2	11	+1	14	100cr	Flamethrower, Pistol, Heavy Armour, Knife
Gunner	5	+3	+3	11	+1	14	100cr	Rapid-fire, Pistol, Heavy Armour, Knife
Armoured Trooper	6	+4	+4	13	+3	14	150cr	Carbine, Combat Armour

* Soldiers listed with Grenades carry both smoke and fragmentation grenades and may choose which type to use at any time. A figure carrying grenades is assumed to have as many of either type as they need for a given game.

SOLDIER GEAR

Each soldier comes with a set of standard gear listed in the notes on the soldier tables. Soldiers may not be given any additional gear from the General Equipment list, although if they lose an item listed in their notes it is replaced for free after the game.

All soldiers have one gear slot; however, soldiers may not take any additional gear from the General Equipment List; this additional gear slot can only be used for gear that is found or purchased during a campaign. See the section on Counting Loot (see page 77) for full details. In the case of weapons or armour, it must be of the same type as the weapons or armour listed in the soldier's notes. In this case, the advanced weapon or armour both replaces their mundane version and fills their one gear slot.

ROBOTS

Whenever a new soldier is recruited, a player may declare that the new soldier is a robot. This has no additional cost and does not change the soldier's stats or equipment. However, the designation 'robot' should be added to the soldier's notes. Robots are immune to the wounding and toxic rules presented in the combat section, and are never effected by gases or low oxygen levels. On the other hand, robots have other vulnerabilities and weaknesses that will become apparent later in the rules. Many of the powers available to captains and first mates can only effect robots or, conversely, have no effect on them.

In terms of appearance, robots can look like anything as long as the figure is near human-sized. Some robots are advanced androids that are only distinguishable from humans on close inspection; others look more like walking appliances.

Captains and first mates may not be robots, though if you like the idea, consider giving them the Cyborg background.

TEMPORARY CREWMEMBERS

While independent crews are limited to ten permanent members (1 captain, 1 first mate, and 8 soldiers), it is sometimes possible to gain additional 'temporary members', through the use of powers, advanced technology, or special scenario conditions. If a crew gains a temporary member, it follows all of the normal rules of a permanent member except that it will participate only in one game. After that game is over, the temporary member leaves the crew.

ALIENS IN STARGRAVE

Aliens in *Stargrave* are broken into two categories: humanoids and non-humanoids. For whatever reason, most of the highly advanced, sentient races in the galaxy are humanoid, in that they have a definable head, torso, two arms, and two legs. The exact look of these parts can vary in the extreme and can include such diverse features as scales, feathers, spines, bone-ridges, small tentacles, etc. As far as these rules are concerned, all of these aliens are treated the same, and players are free to represent all of the members of their crew as whatever humanoid, alien species they wish.

Of course, the *Stargrave* galaxy also includes numerous non-humanoid alien species. In most cases, these aliens will be included in scenarios as 'uncontrolled creatures', and a sample of these are found in Chapter Six: Bestiary (see page 139. Future supplements may include specific aliens with fixed stats and abilities that can be included in a crew.

That said, players should not feel bound by these categories. If you've got a weird alien figure that you really want to include in your crew, that is fine. Use the stats for a normal soldier (or for your captain or first mate if you wish) and make sure you inform your opponent what exactly the figure represents before you start a game. In general, players should try to get figures that roughly match the character they represent, but this should never get in the way of having fun and collecting the miniatures you want.

GENERAL EQUIPMENT LIST

In *Stargrave*, weapons, armour, and equipment are broken down into the classes listed below. The specific weapon inside a class makes no difference. Thus, in game terms, there is no difference between a laser pistol and a pistol that fires explosive bullets; they are both just pistols.

Some weapons have **Damage Modifiers**. This modifier is added or subtracted to the Damage inflicted after the winner of the combat has been determined. Full rules for how each of these weapons work is found in Chapter Two (see page 59).

No figure may ever wear more than one type of armour at a time.

EQUIPMENT

Deck

Also known as a 'cyberdeck' or 'keyboard', these small personal computers help in unlocking data-loot counters. Any figure carrying a deck receives +6 on their rolls to unlock data-loot.

Filter Mask

This mask, which is often integrated with a helmet, includes a compressed oxygen supply. Figures wearing filter masks are never affected by gases or low oxygen levels.

Medic Kit

A figure carrying a medic kit may spend an action to attend to any figure within 2", provided that neither figure is in combat. This action can replace the move action. The recipient figure is immediately cured of any toxins, immediately recovers from stun, and is no longer treated as wounded (unless it loses additional Health later, of course). The medic kit has no effect on robots. There is no limit to how often a medic kit can be used during a game.

Picks

The common slang-term for a small tool-kit designed to break through physical locks and restraints and useful for unlocking physical-loot counters. Any figure carrying picks receives a +6 on their rolls to unlock physical-loot.

WEAPONS

Unarmed

If a model ends up with no weapons, it can fight as normal but suffers -2 Fight and a -2 Damage modifier. Creatures that have no weapons listed in their notes fight with natural weapons, thus are never counted as unarmed.

Knife

This is a knife or other small weapon of last resort. In all likelihood, the knives carried by crew members feature some blade enhancement such as a mono-filament, super heating, electro-discharge, etc. Knives have a -1 Damage modifier. The first knife carried by a figure does not take up a gear slot, so everyone can carry a knife and still have their full complement of gear slots.

Hand Weapon

This includes any kind of weapon that is purpose-built for hand-to-hand fighting on the modern battlefield. It includes powered-blades, electro-staffs, fire-flails, etc. Since the damage inflicted by such weapons rarely relies on the personal power of the wielder, the specific size of the weapon makes little difference, and this category includes light weapons such as fencing swords, as well as giant, two-handed shockhammers. Hand weapons take up one gear slot and have no Damage modifier.

Pistol

The preferred weapon for close-quarter shoot-outs, the pistol is a one-handed firearm. There is an almost infinite variety of pistols, and while lasers and chemically propelled slug-throwers remain the most common, pistols firing wire, flechettes, shaped-plasma, and numerous other projectiles are available. Pistols take up one gear slot, have a maximum range of 10", and have no Damage modifier.

Carbine

The most common weapon seen on the battlefield is the carbine. This includes blaster carbines, wave guns, razor-throwers, and numerous other types, but they all essentially perform the same purpose: killing the enemy at a decent range. Carbines take up two gear slots, have a maximum range of 24", and have no Damage modifier.

Shotgun

These firearms trade some of the range of the carbine for greater hitting power. Shotguns take up 2 gear slots, have a maximum range of 12", and have a +1 Damage modifier. Any figure that normally carries a carbine may trade it for a shotgun instead. This includes all soldiers.

Rapid-fire

These heavy weapons are capable of extremely high rates of fire. When making a Shooting attack, a figure armed with a rapid-fire may either make two Shooting attacks at two separate targets that are within 2" of one another, or one Shooting attack with a +2 Damage modifier. If this figure has two actions available, it may use both of them and make two Shooting attacks at two different targets that are with 2" of one another, both with a +2 Damage modifier. A rapid-fire takes up 3 gear slots and has a maximum range of 24".

A figure carrying a rapid-fire also suffers -1 Move, unless they are wearing heavy armour or combat armour, which includes support harnesses for such weapons.

Grenade – Fragmentation

This grenade is thrown at a target point and has a maximum range of 6". All figures within 1.5" of the target point immediately suffer a +3 Shooting attack. A bag of grenades takes up one gear slot. A fragmentation grenade template is included in the back of the book (see page 170).

Grenade – Smoke

This grenade is thrown at a target point and has a maximum range of 6". It produces a thick, circular cloud of smoke 4" in diameter and 3" high. No line of sight may be drawn through this smoke. At the end of each turn, after the turn on which the grenade was thrown, roll a die: on a 1–5 the smoke dissipates and is removed from the table. A bag of grenades takes up one gear slot. A smoke grenade template is included in the back of the book (see page 170).

GRENADES

Soldiers listed with Grenades carry both smoke and fragmentation grenades and may choose which type to use at any time. A figure carrying grenades is assumed to have as many of either type as they need for a given game. Full rules for throwing and using grenades can be found on page 58.

Grenade Launcher

A grenade launcher increases the range of grenades to 16". However, they are inherently inaccurate, so all rolls to hit a target point are at -1 when using a grenade launcher. A figure carrying a grenade launcher also counts as carrying both types of grenades (fragmentation and smoke). Grenade launchers take up three gear slots.

Flamethrower

This class of weapon, which includes plasma weapons and acid-spewers, sprays out a jet of burning or corrosive plasma, using the template found at the back of the book (see page 171). Flamethrowers take up two gear slots, and a figure carrying one suffers -1 Move, unless they are also wearing heavy or combat armour, which includes a support harness.

Flamethrowers have a +2 Damage modifier. Additionally, targeted figures wearing light or heavy armour do not gain the benefit of that armour, so subtract -1 armour from figures in light armour and -2 armour from those in heavy armour. Combat armour still gets its full benefit. Only count solid cover when determining cover for a figure targeted by a flamethrower attack.

ARMOUR

Light Armour

Light armour generally consists of some kind of tactical vest or breast plate that protects the vital organs. It may also include light protection for the head, knees, and elbows, though this is more to protect against bumps than enemy weapons. A figure wearing light armour receives +1 Armour.

Heavy Armour

This represents any type of heavier armour, and generally includes a hardened breast plate, helmet, and arm and leg greaves. While it affords good protection, it is bulky and heavy. A figure wearing heavy armour receives +2 Armour and -1 Move.

Combat Armour

Rare, expensive, and difficult to maintain, combat armour is the ultimate personal protection on the battlefield. Not only does it provide full-body protection and its own air supply, it also has powered limbs and support to offset its immense weight. A figure wearing combat armour receives +4 armour. Combat armour takes up two gear slots; however, a figure wearing combat armour also counts as carrying a hand weapon, a pistol, and a filter mask, as these are integrated into the armour.

Before the start of any game in which the figure with combat armour participates (including the first), a captain must pay 50cr for each suit of combat armour in their crew, in order to maintain and power the suits. If the suit belongs to a captain or first mate, the suit can be exchanged for something else if the fee isn't paid. If the suit belongs to a soldier, and the fee isn't paid, this soldier may not participate in the coming game – though in this case the soldier may be temporarily replaced by either a Recruit or Runner.

Shield

Shields are rarely seen on the battlefield since most firearms and hand weapons will cut right through them. Thus a normal shield offers no benefit. There are some advanced technology and alien designs that are useful; however, as these can only be obtained when playing a campaign, those specifics are not discussed there. Shields take up one gear slot, but a figure carrying a shield may not carry any weapon that takes up more than one slot (carbines, grenade launchers, etc.)

ARMS AND ARMOUR SUMMARY

GENERAL WEAPONS TABLE

Weapon	Damage Modifier	Maximum Range	Gear Slots	Notes
Unarmed	-2	-	-	-2 Fight
Knife	- 1	-	1	
Hand Weapon	-	-	1	
Pistol	-	10"	1	
Carbine	-	24"	2	
Shotgun	+1	12"	2	
Rapid Fire	+2	24"	3	2 targets, -1 Move unless wearing heavy armour or combat armour.
Grenade – Fragmentation	-	6"	1	3" diameter Damage
Grenade – Smoke	-	6"	1	4" diameter smoke
Grenade Launcher	Grenade	16"	3	-1 Shoot
Flamethrower	+2	Template	2	-1 Move unless wearing heavy armour or combat armour. Target Armour and Cover modifiers (see page 32).

ARMOUR TABLE

Armour	Armour Modifier	Gear Slots	Notes
Light Armour	+1	1	
Heavy Armour	+2	1	- 1 Move
Combat Armour	+4	2	50cr upkeep fee. Includes hand weapon, pistol, and filter mask.
Shield	-	1	May not carry any weapon that takes up 2 or more gear slots.

CHAPTER TWO
THE RULES

Now that you've got your captain and crew assembled, it is time to start your adventures in the Ravaged Galaxy. This chapter covers all of the basic rules for the game, including setting up the table, moving, fighting, using powers, and how to control the alien creatures and pirates that often appear in the middle of an operation.

SETTING UP THE TABLE

The first step in any game of *Stargrave* is to set up a great-looking table filled with terrain. The easiest way to do this is to turn to Chapter Five and select one of the listed scenarios, either by rolling randomly or simply agreeing with your opponent which one to play (see page 119). This will tell you what kind of terrain to use and how to place it on the table, where or how to place loot, what kind of alien creatures might be wandering around, and what special rules, if any, are in effect.

Alternatively, you can ignore the scenarios and just play a 'standard' game. In a standard game, the players should take the terrain they have available and set it up on the table in a mutually agreeable fashion. The galaxy is a hugely diverse place, so any kind of terrain will work – tropical jungle, a shanty town in the desert wastes, the ruins of a vast starship, whatever. The key when setting up terrain is to use a lot of it. The independent crews have to keep a low profile to survive, so they almost never fight 'in the open'. Really though, more terrain just makes for more fun and interesting games. The denser the terrain, the more places there are for figures to hide, use for cover, and dash between. Without a lot of terrain, the game will quickly turn into a static firefight with little manoeuvring.

As a guideline, when setting up the terrain, it should never be possible for a figure to see from one side of the table to the opposite edge. In fact, in most cases, it shouldn't be possible for a figure on the ground to draw line of sight to any point more than a foot or two away.

SELECT TABLE EDGES

Once all of the terrain has been arranged on the table to everyone's satisfaction, each player should roll a die. The player that rolls highest should select their starting table edge. If there is only one other player, that player takes the edge opposite. If there are more than two players, then the second player should select their starting edge, and so on.

In games played on very small tables, say 2' x 2', it might be better for players to select starting corners, instead of table edges, as this makes better use of the available space for paying a game. Four-way games played on 3' x 3' tables might also consider using corners instead.

Once all of the edges or corners have been assigned, the player that chose first should place all of the members of their crew within 2" of their starting edge, but at least 6" away from any other edge. If using corners, all members of the crew should be placed within 5" of the starting corner.

PLACE LOOT TOKENS

Once all of the figures are on the table, it is time to place loot tokens. The acquisition of these tokens is the main objective in most games of *Stargrave*. Loot tokens come in two varieties: data-loot and physical-loot. Players should make it easy to identify which type of loot token is which.

To start, place one loot token in the exact centre of the table. Roll a die to determine its type: on 1–10 place a data-loot token; on 11–20 place a physical-loot token. To make the game more fun, it is best if the centre of the table is a hard to access, or at least a hard to see, location. No figure should ever be able to draw line of sight to this token without first making a move.

Then, starting with the player who placed their figures on the table last, the players should take turns placing additional loot tokens. Each player must place one data-loot and one physical-loot token on the table. A token may be placed anywhere so long as it is over halfway across the table from the placing player's starting table edge, and is at least 6" away from any other loot token. Remember to count vertical distance when measuring the distance between loot tokens.

Full rules for loot tokens are presented later in this chapter (see page 64).

Once all of the terrain, figures, and loot tokens are in place, you are ready to start the first turn!

···· THE TURN ····

Games of *Stargrave* are divided into turns. During each turn, players will have a chance to move all of the figures in their crews.

INITIATIVE

At the beginning of each turn, all players should roll a die. The player who rolls highest is the **Primary Player** for that turn. The player who rolls the next highest becomes the Secondary Player for the turn, and so on. Ties should be re-rolled.

PHASES

Every turn is divided into four phases: the **Captain Phase**, the **First Mate Phase**, the **Soldier Phase**, and the **Creature Phase**. Once all four phases have been completed, the turn is over.

Assuming the game is not over at this point, the players should once again roll for Initiative and begin another turn.

The Captain Phase

The turn begins with the Captain Phase; in which the primary player activates their captain and up to three soldiers of their choice that started the phase within 3" and line of sight of the captain. The player may activate these figures in any order; the captain does not have to activate first. The secondary player then activates their captain and up to three soldiers. This continues until all players have activated their captains. If a player no longer has a captain on the table, they may not activate any figures in this phase.

The First Mate Phase

Once the Captain Phase is complete, the turn moves to the First Mate Phase, which is very similar. In this phase, the primary player activates their first mate and up to three soldiers of their choice within 3" and line of sight of the first mate. These soldiers may not have been activated in the Captain Phase – figures may only be activated once per turn, unless some special effect specifically says otherwise. Again these figures may be activated in any order. The secondary player then activates their first mate and up to three soldiers, and so on until all first mates have activated in the phase. If a player no longer has a first mate on the table, they may not activate any figures in this phase.

The Soldier Phase

After the First Mate Phase comes the Soldier Phase. The primary player activates any remaining soldiers that have not yet activated in the turn. These soldiers are activated one at a time, in whatever order the player wishes. The secondary player then does the same, and so on until all players have activated all of their remaining soldiers.

The Creature Phase

Finally, the turn ends with the Creature Phase. During this phase all uncontrolled creatures – such as alien monsters or pirates – are activated in a manner specified by their rules.

Creatures that are members of a crew, either temporarily or permanently, count as soldiers for the purposes of activation, and thus will activate in one of the first three phases of the turn.

ACTIVATION

When a figure is activated, it may perform two actions. One of those actions can normally only be a move action. The other action can consist of a second move, fighting, shooting, using a power, or any of the special actions listed elsewhere in this book. It does not matter if a figure moves with its first or second action. For example, a figure may fire a carbine and then move, or move and then use a power. While every figure must activate during a turn, it is not required to take any or all of its actions. It is fine for a figure to activate and do nothing, or to use a power and not move. There are situations in which a figure will only be allowed to perform one action. In this case, it can be any action the figure is allowed to take, it doesn't have to be a move. There are a few actions that are allowed to replace a figure's move action; these will be noted. There are also a few things listed as 'free actions', meaning that a figure can perform the stated task without using any actions.

Just a reminder, when activating soldiers in either the Captain or First Mate Phase, it is those soldiers within 3" of the captain or first mate at the beginning of the phase, and not after the captain or first mate has moved. Thus a player may not move their captain and then activate a soldier who is now within 3", who was not within 3" before the captain moved.

In any case, a figure must perform all of its actions before another figure is activated, unless using group activation.

GROUP ACTIVATION

Group Activation is a special case, distinct from the normal activation explained above. Using a group activation allows the player to circumvent the normal activation rule that each figure must complete all of its actions before another figure is activated.

A player may declare a group activation during either the Captain or First Mate Phase. In this case, a player must move all of the figures activating in that phase before any of the figures complete a second action. After all of the figures move, each one may take their second action in whatever order the controlling player chooses. Thus, if a player declared a group activation during the Captain Phase, it is possible for a player to move their captain and up to three soldiers. The captain could then use a power, followed by the three soldiers each taking their second actions in turn.

If a player chooses to use group activation, each figure being activated must move as its first action; it cannot perform any other action beforehand. Also, if using group activation, all figures that are going to be activated in that phase must be part of the group activation. For example, it is not permissible to move a first mate and one soldier, complete their actions, and then activate a second soldier.

There are only a few instances where using a group activation is useful. The most common is to allow multiple figures to gang up on a specific enemy in hand-to-hand combat, although there are also occasions where it is useful to rearrange the positions of various figures to achieve better line of sight, or to allow figures to move past one another through tight confines.

STAT ROLLS

During the turn, a figure may be called upon to make a roll using one of its stats to accomplish a feat that is not covered by any of the general rules. In these cases, a figure will be told to make a **Stat Roll**, such as a Will Roll or Fight Roll, with a **Target Number** of X, where X is equal to the difficulty of the feat being attempted. This will usually be written like this: 'Make a Will Roll (TN16)'. In these situations, the player simply rolls a die and adds the appropriate stat. If the total is equal to or greater than the target number, the figure has succeeded in the task. If the total is less, it has failed.

For example, during a scenario, players may be required break open a door in order to reach some loot. To open the door, a figure must be adjacent to it and spend an action trying to break the lock by making a Fight Roll (TN14). So, the player spends an action, rolls a die, and then adds the figure's Fight stat to the result. If this total is equal to or greater than 14, the figure has successfully broken open the door.

In theory, a scenario can ask for any stat for a Stat Roll. For stats that are not listed with +/- (i.e. Movement, Armour, and Health), just roll and add the figure's current stat. In the case of Health, it is the figure's current Health, not their maximum starting Health. If a character has a split stat, use the character's current stat.

AUTOMATIC SUCCESS AND FAILURE & MAXIMUM BONUSES

Whenever a figure makes a Stat Roll, an unmodified roll of 20 is *always* a success. This is true even if the roll, after modifiers, still falls short of the target number. Conversely, an unmodified roll of 1 is *always* a failure. An unmodified roll means that this is the number showing on the die, before any modifiers are taken into account.

When a crew member makes a die roll of any type, including Stat Rolls, Combat and Shooting Rolls, Activation Rolls, etc., the figure may never have a total bonus greater than +10. If any combination of a figure's stats and modifiers results in a bonus above +10, treat the total as +10 instead.

For example, a captain with Fight +5, using combat drugs (Fight +1), and an Advanced Technology Hand Weapon (+1 Fight), with two supporting figures (+4 Fight) is in combat with an enemy. They would normally receive a bonus of +11 to their roll. However, this is capped to +10.

MOVEMENT

Any time a figure takes two or more actions during its activation, one of those actions must be movement (with a are a few exceptions, noted elsewhere). The first time a figure moves in a phase, it may move up to its Move stat in inches. If a figure chooses to perform a second movement action during the phase (or even a third in rare occasions), it may move up to half its Move stat in inches. Thus, a figure with a Move stat of 5 can use two actions to move 7.5", or, if it has somehow acquired a third action, 10".

Movement does not have to be in a straight line, and the path taken by a figure can include as many turns as desired. However, the maximum movement distance is calculated off the actual ground covered by the figure, including all vertical distance.

Remember, when moving figures, if you measure from the front of the base, it is the front of the base that moves the maximum distance and the rest of the figure should be placed behind this point, or, to put it another way, don't measure from the front of a base, and then place the back of the base at the end of the measurement – thus gaining the size of the base as 'extra' movement.

FIGURE FACING

Figures in *Stargrave* can always see in all directions and can turn to face any direction at any time. This doesn't require an action and can be done outside of a figure's activation.

OBSTRUCTIONS

Movement is simple when figures are moving down roads or through open terrain, but it becomes more difficult when faced with walls, mounds of rubble, or thick brambles. Unless specifically stated by a scenario, all terrain in *Stargrave* may be climbed. Figures are allowed to climb or move over any obstacle at a cost of 2" for every 1", or partial inch, of height. Terrain such as stairs and ladders that were specifically built to be climbed do not suffer from this penalty. Figures move their full amount when climbing them.

Climbing may occasionally lead to awkward situations where a figure ends its movement clinging to the side of a building or rock, where it is impossible to place the miniature. In such a case, just leave the figure at the bottom of the wall and place a small die next to it displaying the number of inches up the wall the figure is currently hanging.

Rough Ground

Rough ground is any kind of ground that is difficult to move upon. It may be represented by areas of battlefield rubble, crater holes, snow, mud, or shallow water. The exact type of rough ground is irrelevant for movement purposes. Every inch, or partial inch, a figure moves through rough ground is counted as 2" for calculating total movement. Thus, a figure with a Move stat of 6 could move 1" through open ground, then 1.5" through rough ground (counting as 4"), and then a final 1" on the other side.

It is worth taking a few minutes before each game to discuss what counts as rough ground as this will help avoid any arguments later.

MOVEMENT INTO COMBAT

Any time a figure moves into contact with an enemy figure (either an opponent or an uncontrolled creature), it is considered to be **In Combat**. Figures in combat do not automatically fight – this still requires one of the figures in the combat to perform a **Fight Action**, but essentially the two figures are locked together for the moment. This is explained further in the section on Combat (see page 49). While a figure is 'In Combat', the only actions it may normally take are to fight or use a power. A figure in combat may not move, shoot, reload, or use gear. This may mean a figure is not able to move during the turn and thus may only take one action.

Forcing Combat

Any time a figure moves within 1" of an enemy figure that is currently able to move (including those figures that have already moved this turn), the enemy figure may choose to **Force Combat**. The enemy figure is immediately moved into contact with the currently active figure and the two are considered to be in combat. This can happen at any point in the path of a figure's movement. This rule means that that a figure cannot run right past an opposing figure, and it allows figures to 'guard' narrow passageways and protect loot and other figures. Note that uncontrolled creatures will *always* force combat if they have the opportunity, unless a creature's description states otherwise.

Figures already in combat or those that are unable to move because of a special effect are not able to force combat.

MOVEMENT OFF THE TABLE

If a figure chooses to move off the table, such as to secure loot or just to retreat from the fight, that figure is now out of the game and may not return. However, figures can never be forced off the table involuntarily, whether by being pushed back from combat, the effects of a power, or any other means, unless another rule specifically allows it. In cases where this would happen, move the figure to the edge of the table and leave it there. Some scenarios have restrictions on where a figure can exit the table, but unless otherwise stated any figure may move off any table edge.

RUN FOR IT!

When a figure is activated, but before it takes any actions, it may declare that it will **Run For It!** The figure may immediately move up to 3" in any direction ignoring all movement modifiers. After this move, its activation ends. A figure may not move within 1" of an enemy figure using this rule. This rule is useful to figures that would otherwise be reduced to almost no movement, such as a figure suffering from toxins who is attempting to carry loot through rough ground.

A figure may not use this rule if it activates in combat, in deep water, or is entitled to no actions when it activates.

JUMPING

A figure may jump any distance provided it moves an equal distance in a straight line before making the jump, and the total movement does not exceed the maximum permitted to the figure for that activation. Jumping distance does count against a figure's total movement. So, a figure that moves 2.5" in a straight line may then jump 2.5" along the same line. It may then continue to move if it has a Move stat greater than 5. Figures may jump a maximum of 1" without any previous movement. Figures may combine their move actions when calculating a jump, so a figure with Move 6, using two actions, could move 4.5" and then jump an equal distance.

FALLING

It is possible that figures standing above the ground could fall over an edge, either by being pushed back in combat or some other special affect. If the figure falls less than 3", the fall has no major effect and the figure can carry on as normal. If the figure falls 3" or more, it suffers Damage equal to the number of inches it fell multiplied by 1.5, rounded down. Thus a figure falling 5" suffers 7 Damage.

A figure may choose to fall voluntarily. This counts as a movement action and any distance fallen counts against the figure's total movement allowance for the activation. If a figure falls more inches than its Move stat, the fall uses up all of its actions. Place it on the ground and end its activation immediately. Figures take Damage as normal if they choose to fall voluntarily.

If a figure is standing closer than 1" to an edge and is pushed back 1" or more towards that edge for any reason, it falls automatically.

SWIMMING

Considering the number different worlds that the crews are likely to visit, sooner or later, somebody is going to end up in the water.

In *Stargrave* water, and all other liquid bodies, are divided into two types: **Shallow** and **Deep**. Shallow water counts as rough ground, but causes no other penalties. All water is assumed to be shallow unless the players or scenario specifically state otherwise.

Deep water is deep enough that it cannot be waded through, so if you want to move in deep water you have to swim. Any time a figure activates while in deep water, it must make a Swimming Roll. This is essentially a special version of a Stat Roll. To make a Swimming Roll, the figure must make a Will Roll (TN5), taking into account the modifiers on the **Swimming Modifiers Table**. If the figure succeeds, it activates as normal. If the figure fails, it receives no actions this turn and also takes Damage equal to the amount by which it failed the Swimming Roll. Robots, figures with a filter mask, or figures that don't have to breathe, do not suffer any Damage from failing a Swimming Roll, but still receive no actions.

SWIMMING MODIFIERS TABLE	
CIRCUMSTANCE	MODIFIER
Carrying physical-loot	-2
Light armour	-2
Heavy or Combat armour	-3
Robot	-3

For example, a pathfinder activates while in deep water. It must immediately make a Will Roll (TN5). It has a Will of +2, but is wearing light armour which provides a -2 modifier. It rolls a die and gets a 4, giving a total of 4. So not only does the pathfinder receive no actions this turn, but it also takes 1 point of Damage.

Deep water is treated as rough ground for the purposes of movement. Any figure fighting while in deep water suffers a -2 Fight (this can apply to both figures in the combat).

Figures that have the Aquatic, Amphibious, Flying, or Levitate special abilities do not have to make Swimming Rolls, suffer no movement penalties in either deep or shallow water, and do not suffer a Fight penalty for being in water. Creatures without any of the above-named special abilities will never intentionally enter deep water and will ignore figures in it for the purposes of determining movement.

No figure may make a Shooting attack while in deep water, but powers (even those that generate a Shooting attack) may be used normally.

COMBAT

Once a figure is in combat with an enemy figure, it may spend one of its actions to fight. It is not required to do this, but generally the only other options are to use a power or do nothing, as figures are not allowed to move, shoot, or use gear while in combat. In a fight, both figures roll a die and add their Fight stat, plus any additional modifiers (to a maximum of +10). The figure with the higher score wins the fight and may inflict Damage on their opponent. To determine Damage, compare the total Fight score of the winning figure, including all modifiers, to the Armour stat of the loser. If the Fight score is greater, subtract the Armour score from it, and the resulting number is the Damage inflicted. This Damage is then subtracted from the Health of the loser (this is explained more fully under Damage, page 59). In the event that the Fight scores are tied, the two figures land their strikes simultaneously – both are considered to be the winner and may inflict Damage on their opponent.

For example, let's say a commando (Fight +4, Armour 11, hand weapon) and a recruit (Fight +2, Armour 10, knife) are currently in combat. The commando uses an action to fight and both figures roll a die. The commando rolls a 13 to which it adds its Fight stat of +4 for a total of 17. The recruit rolls a 7 and adds their Fight +2 for a total of 9. Since the commando's total score of 17 beats the recruit's score of 9, the commando has won the fight. To determine the Damage, the commando takes their total Fight score of 17 and subtracts the recruit's Armour stat of 10 to reveal that 7 points of Damage have been inflicted. This Damage is immediately subtracted from the recruit's current Health total.

Once a winner has been determined and any Damage inflicted, the winner of the fight has a decision to make. They can either have the two figures **Remain in Combat**, or they can **Push Back** either their own figure or their opponent's by 1". This move must be 1" directly away from the opposing figure. This move is not affected by rough terrain, though you can't push back through walls or other barriers. It is possible for a figure to be pushed over an edge in this manner. No figures can force combat on a figure that is pushed back as the result of combat. A figure cannot force combat against an opposing figure that just pushed it back, or that pushed back from combat with it, unless the opposing figure subsequently moves closer. Uncontrolled creatures will always choose to stay in combat unless a specific rules says otherwise.

MAXIMUM ARMOUR

The maximum Armour Stat that any crewman can reach is 14. If any combination of gear, bonuses, or modifiers would take Armour over 14, treat it as 14.

If the winner decides to push back either figure, the figures are no longer considered to be in combat. If the figure that initiated the fight still has another action to use in this activation, it may now do so, remembering that, in most cases, this action can only be movement, as the figure will already have taken one non-movement action in this activation. If the fight was a tie, neither figure is moved, and they remain in combat. If a figure wins a fight against one figure, but is currently also in combat with another, it may not choose to move back, it may only remain in combat or push back its opponent.

Winning a fight and pushing a figure back is generally the only way for a figure to escape from being in combat without the use of a power.

So, to determine the outcome of a fight, follow these steps in this order:

1. Both figures roll a die.
2. Both figures add their Fight stat and any other Fight bonuses (e.g. Power bonuses or friendly figures also in combat).
3. Determine the winner of the combat by comparing Fight scores.
4. Apply Damage modifiers (such as -1 for knives) to the winner's final Fight score.
5. Subtract the opponent's Armour from this total.
6. Apply any Damage multipliers (some rare creatures do x2 or even x3 Damage; occasionally damaged is halved).
7. If the final total is greater than 0, subtract that many points from the loser's Health. If it is 0 or negative, no Damage is done.
8. The winner now has the choice to remain in combat or push either itself or its opponent back by 1".

MULTIPLE COMBATS

During the course of a game, it is quite possible that a group of figures will end up clustered together, and figures will be in combat with two or more enemy figures at the same time.

Although this may seem confusing at first, it is actually pretty simple to unravel. When a figure in combat with multiple opponents spends an action to fight, it must first nominate which opposing figure it is fighting. The fight is then carried out in the normal way, with the addition of the following modifier:

MULTIPLE COMBAT MODIFIER TABLE		
CIRCUMSTANCE	MODIFIER	NOTES
Supporting Figure	+2	Every friendly figure also in combat with the target figure and not in combat with another figure gives a +2. This is cumulative, so three eligible supporting figures would grant a +6 modifier. Note that only one figure per combat may end up with a modifier from supporting figures, so if both figures are eligible for a +2 modifier they cancel each other out and both figures fight at +0. Similarly, if one is eligible for a +4 modifier and the other for a +2, the first fights at +2 and the second at +0. A figure may never claim more than +6 from supporting figures.

Let's look at some examples.

Example 1

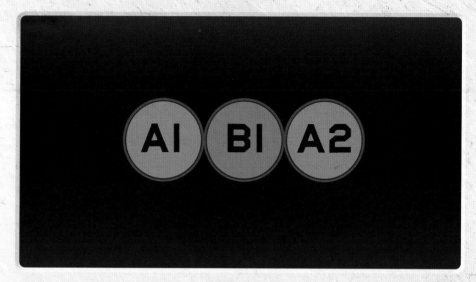

Here, if either A1 or A2 spends an action to attack B1, they will get a +2 modifier as there is another member of the warband in combat with B1 and not in combat with anyone else. B1 may attack either A1 or A2 figure but, again, whichever A figure is attacked will receive a +2 modifier.

Example 2

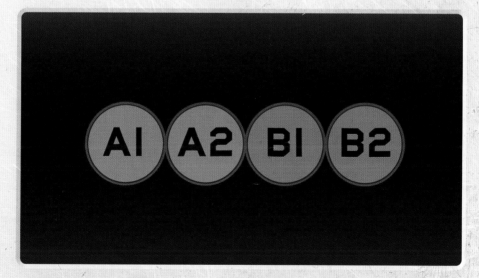

In this example, A2 and B1 are in combat and either may use an action to fight the other. Neither would receive a modifier as neither A1 nor B2 is in combat with an enemy figure.

Example 3

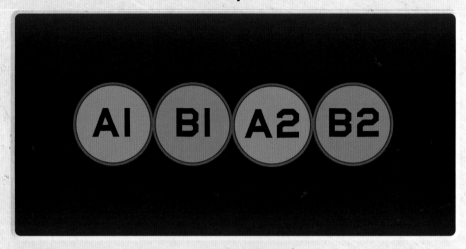

This example is a bit more complicated but, again, no figure would be eligible for the modifier. A1 may attack B1, but since A2 is also in combat with B2, it is unable to provide support. If A2 attacked B1, both figures would count as being in combat with another enemy figure and each would normally receive a +2 modifier. However, as the bonus would apply to both figures, it cancels itself out and they fight as normal.

Example 4

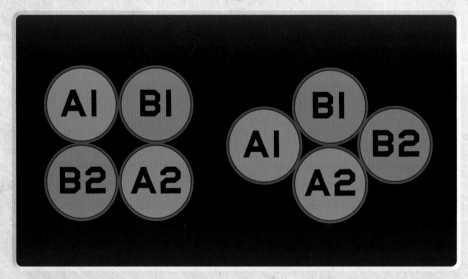

Both of these arrangements also work out so that no figure would actually receive a bonus when fighting any other figure, as any figure that might support an attack is also in combat with another enemy figure, or if B1 and A2 fight, they would both receive support which would cancel out.

Example 5

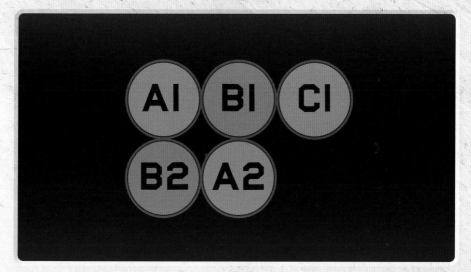

In this example, which might seem confusing at first, an uncontrolled creature (C1) has joined the fight. It is not on anyone's side. If C1 attacks B1, it is not eligible for the modifier, as even though B1 is in combat with two other enemy figures, those enemy figures are themselves both in combat with an enemy figure (B2). In fact, the only situation in which a figure in this combat would be eligible for a modifier is if either A1 or A2 attacks B1. In that situation, they would receive a +2 modifier because C1 is also in combat with B1 and otherwise unengaged. Technically C1 is not 'friendly' to A1 or A2, but since they both want to see B1 dead, it counts.

Combats in *Stargrave* can get messy and turn into big brawls. Just remember a few key points and you should not have any trouble dealing with these situations.

- Only two models – the attacker and the declared target – are *actually fighting*.
- Only these two models can win or lose the fight and suffer Damage.
- They will be supported by any friendly models who are also in combat with the model they are fighting and not in combat with any additional enemy. This support does not require the supporting figure to spend an action.
- Modifiers granted by supporting figures cancel out, so there will never be a case in which both figures receive a bonus to their Fight because of friendly figures in the combat.
- The maximum bonus that any warband member can have to its Fight Roll in a combat is +10.

SHOOTING

If a figure is armed with a pistol, carbine, shotgun, or rapid-fire, it may spend an action to make a Shooting attack (attacks with flamethrowers and grenades still count as shooting attacks but are treated different and explained later, see pages 57–58). Before declaring a Shooting attack, a figure should check that its target is both **In Range** and **In Line of Sight**. To check range, simply measure the distance from the shooter to the target, and compare that to the maximum range of the weapon. Line of sight is a bit trickier to determine. The easiest way is to put your eye down as close to the shooting figure as possible and see if you can see its target. Failing that, you can use string or a laser pointer to draw a line between the shooter and target to see if anything is in the way. If any part of the target figure's head or torso is visible, it is considered to be in line of sight.

Once range and line of sight have been confirmed, a Shooting attack is resolved in a similar way to melee combat. Both the shooter and the target figure roll a die. The shooter adds its Shoot stat to the roll, while the target adds its Fight stat. Any additional modifiers are then added. Once both figures have a final score, the two are compared. If the shooter has the higher score, then the shot hits the target and Damage is determined. If the target has the higher score or the scores are equal then the shot has missed – either the shooter's aim was off, or the target was able to duck out of the way in the nick of time.

Damage is determined in exactly the same way as it is in melee combat. The shooter takes its final Shoot score and subtracts the target's Armour stat. If the result is a positive number, that is the amount of Damage inflicted. If the target takes 4 or more points of Damage, it is also Stunned (see page 59).

For example: a commando with a Shoot stat of +3 fires their carbine at a recruit with Fight +2. The recruit is standing in the open and there are no other modifiers. The commando rolls an 8 and adds their Shoot stat of +3 for a total of 11. The recruit rolls a 2 and adds their Fight stat of +2 for a total of 4. The commando has scored higher and thus has hit their target. We take the commando's total score of 11, and subtract the recruit's Armour 10, to see that 1 point of Damage has been done to the recruit.

Figures in combat may not make a Shooting attack.

If a figure uses a power that generates a Shooting attack, that attack follows all of the same rules, except the figure does not apply its Shoot stat to the roll. Instead it should apply the bonus listed in the power. So if a Mystic activates their Dark Energy power, it would roll a die and add +5 to the roll, ignoring their Shoot stat. The target would roll and add their Fight Stat plus any modifiers listed below. A figure can activate a power that generates a Shooting attack while in combat.

MODIFIERS TO SHOOTING

Modifiers to Shooting are expressed as bonuses to the target's Fight die roll. These modifiers apply to all Shooting attacks unless otherwise stated. Note that if an enemy figure would count as intervening terrain or as cover, line of sight is blocked. Essentially, you may not shoot through or over one enemy figure to hit another one.

SHOOTING MODIFIER TABLE

CIRCUMSTANCE	MODIFIER	NOTES
Intervening Terrain	+1	Every piece of intervening terrain between the shooter and the target gives a +1. This is cumulative, so three pieces of intervening terrain provide a +3 modifier. Note that if the target is in base contact with a terrain piece it counts as cover instead of intervening terrain. If a shooter is in base contact with a terrain piece, it does not count as intervening terrain, though it may block line of sight.
Hasty Shot	+1	The shooter previously moved during this activation.
Cleared Jam	+1	The shooter previously cleared a jam during this activation.
Light Cover	+2	The target is in contact with solid cover (e.g. rocks, walls, thick wood, barricades, heavy machinery, other figures) that covers part of its body, or with soft cover (e.g. bushes, undergrowth, barbed wire, fences) that obscures half or more of its body.
Stunned	+2	The target is currently Stunned.
Heavy Cover	+4	The target is in contact with solid cover that covers half or more of its body.
Large Target	-2	The target is particularly tall or unusually broad. This normally only applies to creatures who will have the 'Large' trait.

A NOTE ON COVER

Determining if a figure is or is not in cover is one of the hardest, most controversial aspects of the game, and there is no way for the rules to encompass every situation. Players are encouraged to remember that the members of the independent crews are a hardened lot, used to having to fight to survive. They know the value of cover and will take advantage of any little scrap they can find. When determining if a figure is in cover, or what level of cover, players should always give the benefit of the doubt to the defender. Chances are they are crouching pretty low to get behind that pipe or tree stump!

SHOOTING INTO COMBAT

Shooting into combat is a legal, if risky, move and even the best marksmen stand an equal chance of hitting a friend instead of a foe. It is impossible to target a figure in combat – but the combat itself may be targeted. If a figure wishes to shoot into the combat, it must first roll randomly to determine which figure in the combat is the actual target of the attack. Once this has been determined, it is too late for the shooter to hold fire – it must carry out a shooting attack in the normal fashion, even if it is against a friendly figure. A figure can target any combat in which it can see at least one figure; in this way, it is possible to hit a figure that is not in line of sight of the shooter.

If the shooting attack generates an area effect or uses a template, such as grenades and flamethrowers, do not roll for a random target. Instead, if at least one figure in the combat is within the area of effect, roll a separate attack against each figure in the combat.

SHOOTING WITH A FLAMETHROWER

When making a shooting attack with a flamethrower, instead of checking for range or line of sight, simply take the flamethrower template from the back of the book (see page 171). Place the pointed end anywhere adjacent to the firing figure's base, and then place the rest of the template pointed however you like. Make a separate shooting attack against every figure that the template touches. Only 'solid cover' should be applied against flamethrower attacks (e.g. a solid wall counts as cover but a fence does not). Note that figures that are completely obscured by solid terrain between them and the shooter do not suffer an attack.

THROWING AND FIRING GRENADES

When throwing or firing grenades of any type, the figure should first nominate a target point. This point does not have to be in line of site, but cannot be beyond the grenade's maximum range and must be reachable via an arc from the shooter. Thus a grenade can be fired or thrown over a wall, but not into a building that has a roof. A grenade can only be shot or thrown through a hole if that hole is in line of sight. So a grenade can be thrown through a window, but only if the window is in line of sight.

The shooter makes a Shoot Roll (TN12), taking into account the modifiers on the **Grenade Attack Modifiers Table** below. If successful, the grenade hits the selected target point. If it was a smoke grenade, place smoke centred on this point. If it was a fragmentation grenade, immediately make separate shooting attacks at +3 against every figure within 1.5" of the target point (calculate cover as drawn from the target point). Remember the blast radius is determined from a point, and not from a specific figure. Thus if a grenade is targeted at the head of a figure, draw the 1.5" radius from the head, not the base, of the figure. Alternatively, a set of grenade templates are included in the back of the book that can be used to place smoke and determine the area of effect of a grenade (see page 170).

If the shooter fails the Shoot Roll, move the target point in a random direction a number of inches equal to the amount by which the shooter failed the roll, to a maximum of 6". If the roll was failed by more than 6, remove the target point; the grenade was either a dud or the shot missed so badly as to be completely ineffectual. If you have a new target point, carry out the attack as normal. In this way, it is possible to throw a grenade and end up accidently hitting friendly figures, or even the thrower if they were close enough to the original target point.

For example, a pathfinder wants to throw a grenade at a target point that is outside its line of sight. It rolls a die and gets a 7, to which is added its Shoot Stat of +3, for a total of 10. Since the roll missed the target number by 2, the target point for the grenade moves 2" in a random direction. Once this new target point has been determined, all figures within 1.5" of it suffer the +3 shooting attack from the fragmentation grenade.

GRENADE ATTACK MODIFIERS TABLE

SITUATION	MODIFIER TO SHOOT ROLL
Target Point is in Line of Sight	+2
Hasty Shot (The figure has already made a Move Action this activation)	-1
Firing with Grenade Launcher	-1

RANDOM DIRECTION

Occasionally, the players will be called upon to determine a random direction. A simple method for this is to roll a d20. Since each facing of a d20 is a triangle, it can serve as a little arrow. Simply look at the direction indicated by the top of the triangle – the point that sits above the number.

EXTREME RESULTS

CRITICAL HITS

Whenever a figure rolls a natural '20' on its combat or shooting die – that is the number rolled on the die is '20' before any modifiers are applied – it has scored a critical hit. This figure automatically wins the combat or hits its target, and does an additional +5 Damage on top of what it would normally do. If both figures in hand-to-hand combat roll natural 20s, they both hit, and both do bonus Damage as normal. If a target in a shooting attack rolls a natural 20, then the shot misses, even if the firer also rolls a natural 20.

WEAPON JAMS

If a figure making a shooting attack rolls a natural 1, then they have either run out of ammunition or their weapon has jammed. Either way, they must spend an action servicing their weapon before they can make another shooting attack with it. This servicing action can replace a figure's mandatory move action.

The Jamming rule only applies to the first Shoot Roll in each flamethrower attack, and only on the initial Shoot Roll when using a grenade launcher. It does not apply to grenades.

···· DAMAGE ····

Whenever a figure takes Damage, whether from combat, shooting, or any other source, the amount of Damage is subtracted from the figure's current Health total. If this takes a figure to 0 Health or less, that figure has been killed and should be removed from the table. In campaigns, the figure may not actually be dead, but is certainly out of the current game.

After the game, a player can check to see what has become of any of their figures that were reduced to 0 Health or less. This is covered in Chapter Three: Campaigns (see page 68).

STUN

Whenever a figure takes 4 or more points of Damage from a single shooting attack – including flamethrower and grenade attacks – it becomes **Stunned**. Essentially, the figure has been badly shocked by the attack and has probably collapsed. The figure's only immediate thought is to seek as much cover as possible while they recover their wits.

Mark the figure as stunned, either with a token of some sort, or by placing the figure on its side. Since a stunned figure is devoting all its effort to maximizing its use of cover, it receives a +2 bonus to Fight Rolls against shooting attacks. The next time this figure activates, remove the token or stand the figure back up. It is no longer stunned, but receives a maximum of one action during this activation.

If another figure moves into combat with a figure that is stunned, immediately remove the token or stand up the stunned figure. The figure is no longer stunned, but suffers -2 Fight on their Combat Roll if the active figure makes a Fight Action in the same activation.

WOUNDED

When any figure is reduced to 4 Health or less, regardless of their starting Health, they are considered **Wounded**. Wounded figures are reduced to one base action per activation instead of the normal two. This one action can be any the figure could normally take and does not have to be movement. Wounded figures also suffer a -2 to *all* die rolls.

Figures that are healed back above 4 Health during the course of the game are no longer wounded.

A figure is never considered wounded if it is at its starting Health; any figure that starts the game with 4 Health or less is not wounded, but will become so upon losing its first point of Health.

Robots are never subject to the wounded rule.

TOXINS

Regardless of whether it is venom delivered by a bite or sting, poison absorbed through touch or consumption, or some kind of horrific gas, the rules for dealing with these toxic substances are exactly the same.

A figure that takes 1 or more points of Damage from a toxic source (or any attack from a figure with the Toxic attribute) is poisoned and reduced to one base action per activation instead of the normal two. This action can be anything; it does not have to be movement.

A figure can be cured of this poison if it receives any form of healing that takes it back up to its starting Health. If the healing does not take the figure back to starting Health, then the poison continues. Otherwise, it may be cured by powers or items that specifically state they cure poison. Poison lasts until the end of a scenario. A figure is assumed to have recovered by the start of the next scenario.

Multiple poisonings have no additional effect; a figure may only be poisoned once at any given time. If a figure is already down to one action per activation due to another rule, then the poison has no additional effect. A figure that is both poisoned and wounded still receives one action.

···· POWERS ····

Captains and first mates may use an action to attempt to activate one of their powers. A figure may never activate more than one power per activation. A figure may activate a power while in combat. There is no limit to the number of times a specific power may be used during a game, unless specifically stated in the description of that power.

As part of the action of using a power, the figure also gets to make a free **Power Move** as explained below.

SUCCESS AND FAILURE

To activate a power, the player announces which power their captain or first mate is attempting to use and the target of that power. The player then rolls a die. If the number rolled is equal to or greater than the activation number of the power, it succeeds. If the roll is less than the activation number, then the power fails to activate, though the figure may still make a power move.

Exertion

After an Activation Roll is made, but before the result is determined, a captain or first mate may choose to **Exert**. Essentially the activator may trade its Health to increase the Activation Roll on a 1-for-1 basis. So, if a captain or first mate failed their roll by 3, they could take 3 Damage and the power would activate.

Strain

Some powers cause immense physical or psychic strain. Whenever a figure activates a power with **Strain** greater than 0, they immediately take Damage equal to the Strain. So, for example, if a Biomorph activates its Adrenaline Surge power, it immediately takes 2 points of Damage. A figure may not attempt to activate a power if the Strain level of that power is equal to or greater than their remaining Health.

A figure may take Damage from both exertion and Strain when activating a power, but can never activate a power if the exertion, Strain, or both would take it to 0 Health or below.

Players should refer to the Chapter Four: Powers (see page 102) for more discussion on individual powers.

POWER MOVE

Whenever a player declares that their captain or first mate will spend an action to use a power, the figure may also make a free 3" move. This move may be made either before or after the power is used and has no effect on the success or failure of the power. This move cannot be made if the figure is in combat, though if the power moves them out of combat, it may then be used. Activating a power and making a power move action counts as the figure's one non-move action for the activation.

A power move is subject to all of the modifiers and limitations of regular movement, such as the penalties for rough ground or climbing. It does not prevent the figure from taking a full move with its other action. So, for example, a captain with two actions could use their first action to move 3" as a power move and attempt to activate a power, then use their second action to move up to their full Move Stat in inches.

A power move cannot be replaced with any other action, even those that can normally replace a move action (such as clearing a jam).

CANCELLING POWERS

If a power has an ongoing effect and no duration is given in the power description, the power lasts until the end of the game. Powers cannot be turned off by the activator unless the power specifically gives that ability, nor is the power ended if the activator leaves the table or is killed (though if the power was used on a figure that is removed from the table, it is no longer relevant).

TARGETING FIGURES IN COMBAT WITH POWERS

If a power generates a shooting attack, and the activator wishes to target a figure in combat, then the activator must roll randomly among the figures in combat to see which figure is actually targeted by the attack. The exception to this is if the activator is itself part of the combat, in which case a shooting attack generated by a power may be targeted on a specific figure, and no random roll is made.

Powers that do not generate shooting attacks may be targeted on figures in combat and always target the intended figure.

COLLECTING LOOT TOKENS

There are two types of loot token: data-loot and physical-loot. Data-loot represents important information, schematics, or digital currency. Physical-loot is money, valuable merchandise, or interesting artefacts. These tokens behave differently in some circumstances.

No loot token may be moved by any means until it is unlocked. If a figure is in contact with a loot token, it may spend an action to attempt to unlock it. This requires the figure to spend an action and make a Will Roll (TN14). On failed result, nothing happens. If successful, the loot token is unlocked and may now be picked up and carried. A figure that successfully unlocks a physical-loot counter may pick it up as a free action as part of the same action, or any other figure may pick it up by spending an action. Data-loot always requires an action to pick it up (download it). Once a loot token is picked up, it should be moved with the figure that is carrying it. A figure may never pick up a loot token if there is an enemy figure within 1".

A figure may only carry one loot token at a time. If it is data-loot, the figure suffers no penalties for doing so. If it is physical-loot, then the figure is slowed while doing so – its Move is halved. Furthermore, it is encumbered, meaning it has -1 Fight and -1 Shoot.

Any time a figure is carrying loot, it may spend one action to drop it. This action can replace the mandatory move action. Move the figure and the loot slightly apart so that they are no longer touching. Any friendly figure may now spend an action to pick up the loot (enemy figures will not be able to pick it up due to the proximity of the figure that just dropped it). If a figure carrying loot is killed, leave the loot token on the spot where the figure fell.

If a figure carrying loot moves off the table via any table edge, the loot has been secured for that crew. This figure and the loot are now out of the game.

Loot has no particular use during the game. In the heat of battle, figures are far too busy fighting for their lives to thoroughly examine what they have found. Chapter Three: Campaigns (see page 77) goes into the niceties of determining the exact nature of loot and the rules for what can be done with it, but this is all handled after the game is over.

It is worth noting that loot tokens are not gear. Any figure may carry one loot token, regardless of the number of gear slots they have available, and loot does not take up a gear slot.

Loot tokens never block line of sight, provide cover, or impede movement (until carried).

CREATURE ACTIONS

The galaxy holds many dangers beyond the pirate fleets and competing independent crews. Many worlds feature deadly flora and fauna that will happily attack anyone who gets too close. Indeed, some alien life-forms are just so different that they view any member of a crew as a threat and attack at once. See Chapter Six: Bestiary for a sample of the most common, famous, and deadly life forms that the galaxy has to offer (see page 139).

The last phase in every turn is the Creature Phase, in which all creatures that are not part of a crew (often called **Uncontrolled Creatures**) take their actions. Creatures that are part of a crew, even if only temporarily, activate as though they were a soldier. Thus, they can be activated along with either a captain or first mate, or they activate in the Soldier Phase.

Like most figures, a creature may perform two actions when it is activated. While more powerful and intelligent creatures may have specific rules for their actions (these will be explained in full in their entries in Chapter Six: Bestiary or in specific scenarios), the lesser, more commonly encountered creatures all follow a simple set of guidelines to determine how they act in any given turn.

Creatures that are not part of a crew will never target or attack another uncontrolled creature. They are not considered to be in combat with each other, even if their bases are touching. Creatures will always force combat with a crew member that moves within 1" of it.

For each creature, starting with the one with the highest Health and working down, the players should go through the following steps to determine its actions. Run through the steps for each of the creature's actions, as situations may change between them (e.g. a creature may be moving towards one target with a movement action when a second, closer target then becomes visible and thus becomes the target of its second movement action).

1. IS THE CREATURE IN COMBAT?

Yes

It will use its action to fight. If it wins the combat, it will choose to stay in combat. If a creature is in combat with more than one opponent, it will attack the one with the lowest current Health.

No

Proceed to Step 2.

2. IS THERE A CREW MEMBER IN LINE OF SIGHT?

Yes

If the creature is armed with a missile weapon, and there is a crew member within range, it will shoot at the closest eligible target. It will take no second action.

If the creature has no missile weapon, it will move as far as it can towards the closest visible figure, climbing obstacles as necessary. If it reaches a crewmember with its first action, it will use a Fight Action against them as its second.

No

Proceed to Step 3.

3. TARGET POINT OR RANDOM MOVEMENT

If the scenario has a Target Point, the creature will make one move towards the Target Point. If there is no Target Point, the creature will move in a random direction. Determine a random direction and move the creature its full Move distance in that direction. If the creature moves into a wall or other obstacle (including the edge of the table – creatures will never leave the table due to random movement), halt its movement at that point. Once this movement is complete, if the creature has an action remaining, check Step 2 once more – if no target has presented itself, the creature's activation ends, and no second action is taken, otherwise, proceed with Step 2 as normal.

•• ENDING THE GAME ••

Games of *Stargrave* can end in several ways. Most commonly, a game ends as soon as the last loot token is moved off of the table. All figures that are still on the table are assumed to make it home safely.

Another way the game can end is if only one player has figures left on the table, either because all of the opposing crew members were killed or have moved off the table. In this case, the player with figures remaining on the table secures all of the loot tokens that are currently being carried by members of their crew. Furthermore, they should roll a die for each unclaimed loot token on the table. On a roll of 15+ they secure that loot as well. On a roll of less than 15, the loot is lost.

In the incredibly rare, but theoretically possible, event that no player has any figures left on the table, the game ends, and all loot tokens left on the table are lost.

Some scenarios may have specific objectives that end the game as soon as they are achieved. These cases will be explained in the specific scenario.

In non-campaign games, the winning player is the one who secures the most loot. In a campaign, there is no specific win condition for most scenarios, and each player is left to decide for themselves whether their captain won or lost the encounter.

CHAPTER THREE
CAMPAIGNS

If you are just getting started, it is probably worth playing a one-off game of *Stargrave* (or two) before diving into a campaign. That way you can get a handle on the rules and a better feel for the different powers without worrying too much about the outcomes of those games. That said, once you've got a feel for the game, most players will probably find it much more satisfying to play a campaign of interconnected games. During a campaign, players can use the loot they collect during games to recruit new soldiers, upgrade their weapons or equipment, and even improve their ship. Also, as captains and first mates advance through a campaign, they will gain experience, allowing them to improve their stats, learn new powers, and become more proficient at using the powers they already know. This chapter provides players with all of the information needed in order to take their captain and crew through a campaign.

After each scenario, each player should follow these steps in this order:

1. Check for injury or death
2. Use Out of Game (A) powers
3. Calculate experience and levels
4. Roll for loot
5. Spend loot

INJURY AND DEATH

The galaxy is a tough place, and death is frightfully commonplace, especially among the independent crews. In a standard game of *Stargrave*, any figure that is reduced to 0 Health is assumed to be dead. In a campaign game, however, a figure reduced to 0 Health is assumed to be 'out of the game' – but not necessarily dead. It may be that this figure has been knocked unconscious, is too badly wounded to continue to fight, or has simply lost their nerve and run away.

The first thing a player needs to do at the end of a campaign game is to check the status of the figures that were knocked out of the game (i.e. reduced to 0 Health or less).

Any figures that were not reduced to 0 Health during a game, start the next game at the full starting Health.

SOLDIERS

For soldiers, this is a simple process: just roll a d20 on the **Soldier Survival Table**.

SOLDIER SURVIVAL TABLE	
D20 ROLL	RESULT
1–4	Dead
5–8	Badly Wounded
9–20	Full Recovery

Dead

The soldier has been killed and should be removed from the Crew Sheet. Any gear this soldier was carrying is lost.

Badly Wounded

The soldier is badly wounded. This figure starts the next game at half of their normal Health (rounded down).

Full Recovery

The soldier recovers quickly from their ordeal and return for the next game at full Health.

CAPTAINS AND FIRST MATES

For captains and first mates, it is a bit more complicated. Roll on the **Survival Table** below to determine the result if one of your command team is knocked out of the game. When rolling for a captain, a player has the option to add +1 to the roll, after the die is rolled.

SURVIVAL TABLE	
D20 ROLL	**RESULT**
1–2	Dead
3–4	Permanent Injury
5–6	Badly Wounded
7–8	Close Call
9–20	Full Recovery

Dead

The figure doesn't survive its injuries. See the section on New Recruits for what to do when your captain or first mate dies (see page 97).

Permanent Injury

The figure suffers an injury that never fully heals. Roll on the **Permanent Injury Table** (see page 71) to determine the exact nature of the permanent injury. Otherwise, the figure returns for the next game at full Health.

Badly Wounded

The figure has received a major injury that will take time to heal. The captain has a choice. The badly wounded figure can either start the next game at half of its normal starting Health (rounded down), or the captain can pay 100cr for medical treatment, or 50cr if there is a medic in the crew. If the captain does not have the appropriate amount, they are allowed to go into debt to pay this fee. However, the captain may not spend any credits until this debt is paid in full. If the fee is paid, the figure starts the next game at full Health.

Close Call

The figure escapes with no major injury, but loses all of the gear it was carrying. Items from the General Equipment List are replaced for free.

Full Recovery

The figure's injuries proved to be relatively minor, and it returns at full strength in the next game.

PERMANENT INJURIES

Whenever a figure receives a permanent injury it should be listed in the figure's notes on the Crew Sheet. If the injury causes a penalty to one of its stats, the player should write that stat as a split stat. So, a captain that goes into the game having a Fight stat of +3, but receives a Crushed Arm permanent injury, should now write their stat as +3/+2.

This is very important for record-keeping purposes. The first number in a split stat is the figures' actual level of ability, and should be used to determine if the figure has reached their maximum potential in a given stat. It will also be the number that corresponds to the level of the captain or first mate (see Experience and Level, page 74). For the purposes of any die rolls pertaining to the stat, however, the second number should be used.

PERMANENT INJURY TABLE

D20 ROLL	INJURY
1–2	Lost Toes
3–6	Smashed Leg
6–10	Crushed Arm
11–12	Lost Fingers
13–14	Never Quite As Strong
15–16	Psychological Scars
17–18	Lingering Injury
19	Smashed Jaw
20	Lost Eye

Lost Toes

The figure has lost one or more toes. They suffer a permanent -2 whenever it has to make a Move Stat roll. This injury can be received twice, with a cumulative effect of -4 to all Move Stat rolls. Any further Lost Toes results must be re-rolled. Note that this penalty doesn't actually affect the Move Stat, just rolls made against the Stat.

Smashed Leg

The figure suffers permanent bone or muscle damage in its leg. They suffer a -1 Move penalty. This injury can be received twice, with a cumulative effect of -2 to Move. Any further Smashed Leg results must be re-rolled.

Crushed Arm

The figure suffers permanent bone or muscle damage in its arm. They suffer a -1 Fight penalty. This injury can be received twice, with a cumulative effect of -2 Fight. Any further Crushed Arm results must be re-rolled.

Lost Fingers

The figure has lost one or more fingers. They suffer a permanent -1 Shoot penalty when using any kind of ranged weapon. This injury can be received twice, with a cumulative effect of -2 Shoot. Any further Lost Fingers results must be re-rolled.

Never Quite As Strong

Due to internal injuries, the figure doesn't quite return to full Health. They start every game at -1 Health. This injury can be received twice, with a cumulative effect of -2 Health. Any further Never Quite As Strong results must be re-rolled.

Psychological Scars

The figure's physical injuries healed fully, but the mental trauma remains. They suffer a -1 Will penalty. This injury can be received twice, with a cumulative effect of -2 Will. Any further Psychological Scars results must be re-rolled.

Lingering Injury

The figure's injury just never quite healed, and they are forced to use drugs, or other expensive medical aids, to reduce the pain. The figure must spend 30cr on these treatments before each game, or start each game at -3 Health. This injury can be received twice – in which case the payment increases to 40cr and the penalty to -4 Health. Any further Lingering Injury results must be re-rolled. A 10cr discount applies to these payments if there is a medic in the crew.

Smashed Jaw

The figure suffered a broken jaw that never quite healed properly. They have some difficulty with speaking, which affects their ability to lead their crew. Whenever this figure activates, they can only activate a maximum of two soldiers in their phase (instead of the normal three). For example, a first mate with a Smashed Jaw could only activate two soldiers in the First Mate Phase. If this injury is received a second time, the number of soldiers that may also activate in the phase is decreased to one. Any further Smashed Jaw results must be re-rolled.

Lost Eye

One of the figure's eyes has been damaged and rendered useless. They suffer a -1 to their Fight Roll whenever they are the target of a shooting attack. If a figure receives two Lost Eye permanent injuries, they are effectively blind, and unable to continue their adventures. Treat them as though they had rolled a 'Dead' result.

EXPERIENCE AND LEVEL

The best part about playing a campaign is watching your captain and first mate grow in power over the course of their adventures. In game terms, this is represented in two ways: **Experience** and **Level**.

EXPERIENCE

Experience represents the knowledge that a crew gains during their adventures in the Ravaged Galaxy. Experience isn't tied to any specific figure, but can be used to buy new levels for the captain and the first mate. Experience is earned through specific in-game achievements as detailed on the **Experience Table** below. Note that many scenarios will also include bonus experience points that can be earned for achieving certain aims within the scenario.

A crew may earn a maximum of 300 experience points per game played.

EXPERIENCE TABLE	
EXPERIENCE	**ACHIEVEMENT**
+30	For each game played with the crew.
+30	If the crew had at least one figure reduced to 0 Health during the game.
+20	For each loot token unlocked by a member of the crew.
+10	For each power successfully activated* by the captain or first mate (to a maximum of +100).
+10	For each member of a rival crew reduced to 0 Health by a member of your crew (to a maximum of +40).
+5	For each uncontrolled creature reduced to 0 Health by the crew (to a maximum of +20).**

* Does not apply if that power results in the unlocking of a loot token (although experience points for unlocking the loot token do apply).
** Does not apply to creatures that have a specific experience reward given in the scenario.

It is useful to jot down experience as it is earned so that it is not forgotten at the end of a game. After each game, the crew should total up the experience it has gained, and add this to the amount with which it began the game. Every full 100 points of experience may now be converted into a level for either the captain or first mate.

LEVEL

Level is a numerical representation of the power of a captain or first mate. Generally, figures of the same (or similar) level will be close to one another in terms of strength, even if their abilities vary wildly. All captains start at Level 15, all first mates start at level 0. Thus a captain is significantly stronger than a first mate. The captain has better stats, more powers, and better activation numbers on those powers. In the same way, a level 30 captain is significantly stronger than a starting captain at level 15.

After each game, a crew can cash in 100 experience points to gain a new level for either its captain or first mate. If it has enough experience points, multiple levels may be bought. So, if a crew has 300 experience points, they may buy 3 levels for either their captain or their first mate, or split that in any way they choose, for example – buying 1 level for the captain and 2 for the first mate. The only limitation is that a captain may never be more than 20 levels higher than a first mate, and a first mate must always be at least 5 levels lower than the captain. Soldiers do not have levels and may not gain them. The only way a soldier can improve is through carrying better gear.

Every time a captain or a first mate gains a level, they also gain an improvement. The exact type of improvement depends on their new level, as seen on the table below.

IMPROVEMENT TYPE PER LEVEL

FIGURE'S NEW LEVEL	IMPROVEMENT
1, 11, 21, 31, 41, 51, etc.	Lower an Activation Number
2, 12, 22, 32, 42, 52, etc.	Improve a Stat
3, 13, 23, 33, 43, 53, etc.	Lower an Activation Number
4, 14, 24, 34, 44, 54, etc.	Lower an Activation Number
5, 15, 25, 35, 45, 55, etc.	New Power
6, 16, 26, 36, 46, 56, etc.	Lower an Activation Number
7, 17, 27, 37, 47, 57, etc.	Improve a Stat
8, 18, 28, 38, 48, 58, etc.	Lower an Activation Number
9, 19, 29, 39, 49, 59, etc.	Lower an Activation Number
10, 20, 30, 40, 50, 60, etc.	New Power or Improve a Stat

Improving a Stat

The figure may improve one of the following stats by +1, up to the maximum shown in brackets: Move (7), Fight (+6), Shoot (+6), Will (+8), Health (25).

Lower an Activation Number

The figure can lower the Activation Number of any power it possess by 1. Any Activation Number may be lowered to 4, but never below 4, regardless of whether it is one of the figure's Core Powers. A figure may not lower the Activation Number on the same power more than once after each game, although they could lower the Activation Number on two different powers if they gained two levels.

New Power

The figure may learn a new power. This can be any power listed in Chapter Four: Powers (see page 102). If the new power is a Core Power for that figure's background, then it has an Activation Number equal to the one listed in the power. If it is not a Core Power then it has an Activation Number equal to the one listed +2. This is true regardless of whether the figure is a captain or first mate. In other words, first mates suffer no additional penalties when learning a new power.

COUNTING LOOT

In one-off games of *Stargrave*, loot is only used to determine the winner. In a campaign, however, loot is a crucial element in the progression and improvement of a crew.

For each loot token a crew managed to secure, they may roll once on the appropriate loot table below. Note that there are different tables for data-loot and physical-loot.

DATA-LOOT TABLE		PHYSICAL-LOOT TABLE	
DIE ROLL	**REWARD**	**DIE ROLL**	**REWARD**
1	75cr	1	Trade Goods (75cr)
2	d20 x 10cr	2	Trade Goods (150cr)
3	150cr	3	Trade Goods (200cr)
4	d20 x 15cr	4	Trade Goods (250cr)
5	250cr	5	Trade Goods (300cr)
6	d20 x 20cr	6	Trade Goods (400cr)
7	Information (75cr)	7	Advanced Weapon
8	Information (100cr)	8	Advanced Weapon
9	Information (125cr)	9	Advanced Weapon
10	Information (150cr)	10	Advanced Weapon
11	Information (200cr)	11	Advanced Weapon
12	Advanced Weapon	12	Advanced Technology (Table 1)
13	Advanced Weapon	13	Advanced Technology (Table 1)
14	Advanced Weapon	14	Advanced Technology (Table 1)
15	Advanced Technology (Table 1)	15	Advanced Technology (Table 2)
16	Advanced Technology (Table 1)	16	Advanced Technology (Table 2)
17	Advanced Technology (Table 2)	17	Advanced Technology (Table 2)
18	Advanced Technology (Table 2)	18	Alien Artefact
19	Secret (200cr)	19	Alien Artefact
20	Secret (200cr)	20	Alien Artefact

CREDITS (CR)

The most basic form of currency in the galaxy is the 'credit'. There is no such thing as a physical credit, it is really just a small packet of data, but it is accepted as 'legal tender' the galaxy over. The player should add the listed amount to the credits total on their Crew Sheet. Credits can be used to hire soldiers, buy advanced technology, and improve a ship. See the next section on 'Spending Loot' for full details (page 97).

INFORMATION

In a high-tech galaxy, information is money, at least to someone. Maybe the information is a list of the members of an organization, banking codes, or even the chemical formula of a specific form of pesticide. Whatever the exact nature of the information, a crew may trade any Information recovered for 20 experience points. This experience does not count against the normal 300 experience point limit on a game. Alternatively, information may be sold for the listed amount of credits.

SECRET

The galaxy is filled with secrets, such as the locations of ancient weapon caches, the star-routes for smuggler runs, and the codes for unlocking alien computers. A secret should be stored on the ship until it is used. A crew may use a secret before any game. If they do, it should be removed from the crew sheet. If the crew recovers the loot token from the centre of the table, they may trade it for any Advanced Weapon, Advanced Technology, or Alien Artefact of their choice, without rolling on any table. If the crew fails to recover the central loot token, then the opportunity is lost. Otherwise, the secret can be sold for the listed amount of credits.

TRADE GOODS

Trade goods represent a huge variety of items that are worth significant amounts of money, but are of little practical value to the independent crews. This includes food, domestic items, artwork, raw minerals, etc. These items can be traded for credits equal to the amount listed.

ADVANCED WEAPON

The crew have discovered some kind of high-tech weapon or design specs to help produce such a weapon. Either way, the crew should make one roll on the **Advanced Weapon Table** to see exactly what they have found. This can be given to any figure that can use the weapon, stored in the ship or sold. To give a soldier an Advanced Weapon, it must be of the same type of weapon that they normally carry. The Advanced Weapon both replaces their normal weapon and takes up their one available gear slot.

All Advanced Weapons are Indestructible. Weapons listed with Extended Range, have their range increased to the distance noted. Weapons with a Damage modifier add this on top of whatever Damage modifier the weapon normally has, so a Shotgun (+1 Damage), does a total of +2 Damage. Some advanced weapons take up fewer gear slots than normal. This is only useful for captains and first mates. While these weapons may be given to a soldier, and thus give them an indestructible weapon, it still takes up their only gear slot. A few weapons modify a figures' stats, in which case the figure should write the stat as a split stat using the modifier.

When an Advanced Technology weapon grants a bonus to the user's Fight Stat, this only applies when the user is making Combat Rolls in hand-to-hand combat. It does not apply when rolling against shooting attacks, unless this is specifically stated.

ADVANCED WEAPON TABLE

Die Roll	Weapon	Cost	Sell
1	Pistol, Extended Range 14"	200cr	80cr
2	Pistol, +1 Damage	250cr	100cr
3	Pistol, +1 Shoot	400cr	200cr
4	Pistol, Extended Range 14" & +1 Damage	400cr	200cr
5	Carbine, Only takes up 1 gear slot	300cr	120cr
6	Carbine, +1 Damage	400cr	160cr
7	Carbine, +1 Shoot	500cr	250cr
8	Carbine, Only takes up 1 gear slot, +1 Damage	500cr	250cr
9	Shotgun, Extended Range 16"	250cr	120cr
10	Shotgun, +1 Damage	300cr	150cr
11	Shotgun, Only takes up 1 gear slot	300cr	120cr
12	Shotgun, +1 Shoot	500cr	250cr
13	Hand Weapon, +1 Damage	300cr	120cr
14	Hand Weapon, +1 Fight	400cr	200cr
15	Rapid Fire, Only takes 2 gear slots	400cr	160cr
16	Rapid Fire, +1 Damage	600cr	300cr
17	Grenade Launcher, +1 Shoot (only applies to roll to hit target point, not rolls against figures).	400cr	160cr
18	Grenades – Fragmentation, +1 Damage (applies to all grenade attacks made by the figure carrying this gear).	400cr	160cr
19	Flame Thrower, +1 Damage	500cr	200cr
20	Carbine, +1 Shoot, +1 Damage, Only Takes up 1 gear slot	1000cr	400cr

ADVANCED TECHNOLOGY

The crews have discovered some kind of high-tech device or design specs to help build such a device. Either way, the crew should make one roll on the appropriate **Advanced Technology Table** to see exactly what they have found. This can be given to any figure that can use the item, stored in the ship, or sold. Unless otherwise noted, all items take up 1 gear slot. When gear is listed with parenthesis (x), the number listed is the number of times the gear can be used before it is exhausted. A full explanation of each item is given below the tables.

ADVANCED TECHNOLOGY TABLE I

DIE ROLL	ITEM	COST	SELL
1	Advanced Technology Deck	160cr	100cr
2	Advanced Technology Picks	160cr	100cr
3	Integrated Filter Mask	160cr	100cr
4	Nano-surgery Kit	300cr	120cr
5	Combat Armour, Advanced Weapon Systems	800cr	300cr
6	Light Armour with Energy Shielding	300cr	120cr
7	Heavy Armour with Energy Shielding	400cr	160cr
8	Energy Shield	400cr	160cr
9	Combat Drugs (2)	100cr	50cr
10	Pain-masker	150cr	75cr
11	Gravity Suppressor	500cr	200cr
12	Jump Pack	500cr	200cr
13	Improved Drone	500cr	250cr
14	Holographic Projector	400cr	100cr
15	Surge Battery	400cr	100cr
16	Robot Repair Kit	300cr	100cr
17	Fragmentation Armour	500cr	250cr
18	Grapplewire	300cr	150cr
19	Anti-toxin (2)	200cr	100cr
20	Psychic Shield	400cr	150cr

ADVANCED TECHNOLOGY TABLE II

Die Roll	Item	Cost	Sell
1	Plasmablaster	300cr	150cr
2	Anti-gravity Patch (3)	200cr	100cr
3	Weapon Cage	200cr	150cr
4	Extended Magazine	300cr	200cr
5	Robot Antenna	400cr	150cr
6	Jet boots	300cr	120cr
7	Gill suit	300cr	120cr
8	Liftgloves	300cr	120cr
9	Hardsuit	400cr	200cr
10	Pulse Disperser	500cr	200cr
11	Neutron Polarity Reverser	1000cr	250cr
12	Hotshift Pack	400cr	200cr
13	Grapplegun	500cr	250cr
14	Robot Scrambler	300cr	150cr
15	Neural Chip	350cr	150cr
16	Swiftsuit	500cr	250cr
17	Ablative Armour Plates	200cr	150cr
18	Data Virus	300cr	100cr
19	Power Selector	300cr	125cr
20	Pistol Belt	300cr	125cr

Ablative Armour Plates

The first two points of Damage taking by this figure from any external source are absorbed by the ablative armour plates. Once two points of Damage have been absorbed, this gear is destroyed.

Anti-gravity Patch

A figure carrying this patch may apply it as a free action to a physical-loot token that it is carrying, or that is within 1". No figure suffers a movement penalty for carrying this loot token. There is enough for three uses.

Anti-toxin

A figure carrying anti-toxin may use it as a free action. Alternatively, they may use an action to apply it to another figure within 1", provided neither figure is in combat. The figure is cured of all toxins and poisons (see page 60). If this gear is found or purchased, there is enough for two doses.

Advanced Technology Deck

This item may only be given to a figure that can normally carry a deck. When making a roll to unlock a Data-loot token, this figure receives +8 to its Will Roll.

Advanced Technology Picks

This item may only be given to a figure that can normally carry picks. When making a roll to unlock a physical-loot token, this figure receives +8 to its Will Roll.

Combat Armour, Advanced Weapon System

This suit of combat armour replaces the integrated pistol with an integrated shotgun; so the figure wearing this armour counts as armed with a shotgun that takes up no additional gear slots. The upkeep cost of this suit of armour is increased from 50cr to 75cr.

Combat Drugs

These drugs may be stored on the ship and used by any non-robot figure before a game. That figure receives +1 Fight and -1 Will. This may not take a figure's total Fight above +6. If found or purchased, there are enough drugs for 2 doses.

Data Virus

Choose one Data-loot token on the table, it does not have to be in line of sight. That loot token now requires a Will Roll (TN26) to unlock. This is a one-use item. After it is used, remove it from the Crew Sheet.

Energy Shield

This shield projects a small force screen. The wearer gains +1 Armour and +1 Fight when rolling against a shooting attack. This bonus against shooting attacks does not stack with armour that also has Energy Shielding, but the +1 Armour does.

Extended Magazine

A figure carrying this piece of gear does not suffer any penalties the first time each game that it rolls a 1 on a shooting attack.

Fragmentation Armour

The player can decide if this is Light armour or Heavy armour when the gear is found or purchased. Once the decision is made, it cannot be changed. This is treated as a normal suit of armour, except that the figure wearing it gets +1 Armour against fragmentation grenade attacks only.

Gill Suit

A figure carrying this gear count as having the Amphibious attribute.

Grapplegun

A figure carrying this item and standing next to a wall may spend an action and make a Shoot Roll (TN10). If successful, the figure may immediately climb up to 8" straight up as a free action. This does not count as a move action, though other figures may force combat if the figure moves within 1".

Grapplewire

Once per game, a figure carrying this gear may force combat with another figure that moves within 3" instead of the normal 1". All other rules to forcing combat apply normally.

Gravity Suppressor

A figure wearing this device never takes any Damage from falling, no matter the distance.

Hardsuit

This protective layer is designed to be worn under armour and helps with some of the shock from being shot. A figure wearing a hardsuit is only stunned if they take 6 or more points of Damage from a Shooting attack.

Heavy Armour with Energy Shielding

Counts as a normal suit of heavy armour, except the figure receives +1 Fight when rolling against a shooting attack.

Holographic Projector

A figure carrying this device receives +1 to their Activation Roll when attempting to activate the Holographic Wall power.

Hotshift Pack

Once per game, a figure carrying this device may make two shots at two different targets using one action with a pistol, carbine, or shotgun. After making these shots, the weapon is rendered inoperable for the rest of the game, and no further shooting attacks may be made with it. If a 1 is rolled for either of these shots then the hotshift pack is destroyed.

Improved Drone

This item does not have to be carried by a figure, it may be stored in the ship. Once per game, if a figure in the crew successfully activates the Drone power, their Drone has +1 Move and +1 Fight. If this Drone is reduced to 0 Health during the game, roll a die. On a 1-4 it was destroyed and should be removed from the Crew Sheet. On any other result, it was only damaged, and may be used again in future games.

Integrated Filter Mask

This filter mask may only be carried by a captain or first mate. Figures wearing filter masks are never affected by gases or low oxygen levels. It takes up 0 gear slots.

Light Armour with Energy Shielding

Counts as a normal suit of light armour, except the figure receives +1 Fight when rolling against a shooting attack.

Jet Boots

Once per game, a figure with this gear may either add +3 Move for one activation or add +10 to a Move Stat Roll. This decision to use this gear may be made after the Stat Roll has been made

Jump Pack

Once per game, a figure wearing a jump pack may make one move in any direction, including vertically, that ignores all movement penalties for rough ground, climbing, or carrying a physical-loot token.

Liftgloves

Once per game, a figure with this gear may add +8 to Fight Stat Roll that has a Target Number (not a Combat Roll). This decision may be made after the Stat Roll has been made.

Nano-surgery Kit

This is an advanced technology medic kit and may be carried by any figure that could normally carry a medic kit. It follows the normal rules for a medic kit, except that the target figure also regains 1 lost point of Health. No figure may gain more than 1 point of Health from Nano-surgery kits each turn.

Neural Chip

A figure carrying a neural chip receives +1 Will.

Neutron Polarity Reverser

Only useable by a captain or first mate. Once per game, the figure may attempt to use the Cancel Power power, even if they do not possess it. Roll for activation as normal, using the base Activation Number, adding the figure's Will Stat to the roll. The figure may not Exert to use this power. If a natural 1 is rolled for the activation, the Neutron Polarity Reverser is destroyed.

Pain-masker

A figure carrying these drugs may use an action to give them to any figure within 1". That figure immediately regains up to 4 lost points of Health. A figure that is already carrying a Medic Kit or Nano-surgery Kit may carry one dose of these drugs without them taking up a gear slot.

Pistol Belt

This belt can hold two pistols. Essentially, a figure wearing this belt can carry two pistols using one gear slot. Additionally, the figure does not suffer the Weapon Jam penalty the first time they roll a 1 on a shooting attack while using a pistol during a game.

Plasmablaster

Once per game, a figure carrying this weapon may make a flamethrower attack, following all of the normal rules (see page 57).

Psychic Shield

A figure carrying this gear is immune to the Suggestion power.

Pulse Disperser

Once per game, a figure carrying this device may activate their Electromagnetic Pulse power as though it had Strain: 0 (instead of Strain: 1).

Power Selector

This device may be used by anyone carrying a pistol, carbine, or shotgun. When making a shooting attack, the figure may decide to suffer a -1 Shoot in order to gain +2 Damage. They must make this decision before the dice are rolled. If a 1 is rolled on a shooting attack in which the power selector has been used, then the power selector is destroyed.

Robot Antenna

Once per game, a figure attempting to activate either the Remote Guidance or Robot Firing power may add +1 to its Activation Roll. The decision to use this device can be made after the Activation Roll.

Robot Repair Kit

A figure carrying this gear may spend an action to restore up to 2 lost points of Health to any robot within 1", provided neither figure is in combat. Alternatively, if the figure carrying the kit uses the Repair Robot power, it restores up to 6 lost points of Health to a robot (instead of the normal 5). No figure may receive the benefits of a Robot Repair Kit more than once in a turn.

Robot Scrambler

If a figure wins a round of hand-to-hand combat with a robot, they may choose to use this device instead of inflicting any Damage. The robot must immediately make a Will Roll (TN20) or shut down. If shut down, the robot is removed from the table as though it was reduced to 0 Health, but does not have to make a Survival Roll after the game. It automatically returns for the next game at full Health.

Surge Battery

Once per game, a figure carrying this device may use the Power Spike power as though it had Strain: 0 (instead of Strain: 1).

Swiftsuit

This skinsuit is designed to be worn under armour. A figure wearing this suit gains +1 Move, but it may not take a figure over Move 7.

Weapon Cage

This gear can be applied to any weapon. That weapon becomes indestructible. This gear does not take up a gear slot, even if used by a soldier.

ALIEN ARTEFACT

The crews have discovered some rare artefact from a non-humanoid civilization. They should make one roll on the **Alien Artefact Table** to see exactly what they have found. Artefacts may only be carried by captains and first mates, stored in the ship, or sold. Alien artefacts take up one gear slot unless otherwise stated. No figure may carry more than one of each type of alien artefact. A full explanation of each item is given below the table.

Die Roll	Item	Cost	Sell
ALIEN ARTEFACT TABLE			
1	Micro Transporter	1000cr	300cr
2	Pickcaster	600cr	200cr
3	Mindshackles	600cr	200cr
4	Dark Energy Crystal	800cr	250cr
5	Data Worm	1000cr	400cr
6	Enhanced Energy Shield	800cr	250cr
7	Robolock	600cr	200cr
8	Sensory Tendrils	500cr	200cr
9	Binding Talisman	600cr	300cr
10	Psychic Resonator	800cr	300cr
11	Flicker Light	600cr	300cr
12	Mindspike	800cr	300cr
13	Phase Manipulator	600cr	250cr
14	Focalizing Crystal	750cr	200cr
15	Garkon Tick	600cr	200cr
16	Reality Distorter	650cr	250cr
17	Razor Derringer	800cr	350cr
18	Hearthrike	1000cr	300cr
19	Blessed Horthath	600cr	350cr
20	Cursed Idress	800cr	200cr

Binding Talisman

Once per game, a figure attempting to activate the Heal power may choose one of the following options. Either they receive +2 on the Activation Roll or the power Heals up to 7 lost points of Health (instead of the normal 5). This decision may be made after the Activation Roll has been made.

Blessed Horthath

Once per game, a figure carrying this artefact may add +2 to the Activation Roll when attempting to activate the Fortune power, this may be decided after the Activation Roll has been made.

Cursed Idress

Once per game, if a figure carrying this device attempts to activate the Puppet Master power they may choose to either gain +2 to the Activation Roll, or treat the power as if it has Strain: 1 (instead of Strain: 2). This decision may be made after the Activation Roll has been made.

Dark Energy Crystal

If a figure carrying this crystal uses the Dark Energy power, that power is treated as having Strain: 0 (instead of Strain: 1).

Data Worm

Once per game, a figure carrying this item can activate Data Jump, Data Knock, or Data Skip without paying the normal Strain cost.

Enhanced Energy Shield

The first time each game that a figure carrying this device activates the Energy Shield power, that shield can absorb the next 4 points of Damage taken instead of 3. Subsequent uses of this power are treated as normal.

Flicker Light

Once per game, if a figure carrying this device attempts to activate the Quick-Step power they may choose to either gain +2 to the Activation Roll, or treat the power as it were Strain: 0 (instead of Strain: 1). This decision may be made after the Activation Roll has been made.

Focalizing Crystal

Once per game, a figure with the Void Blade power can use this crystal to successfully activate that power without having to make an Activation Roll. (No experience points are gained for activating a power this way.)

Garkon Tick

Once per game, if a figure carrying this device attempts to activate the Adrenaline Surge or the Armour Plates power they may choose to either gain +2 to the Activation Roll, or treat the power as if it were Strain: 1 (instead of Strain: 2). This decision may be made after the Activation Roll has been made.

Hearthrike

A figure carrying this artefact never suffers Armour Interference penalties while wearing light armour.

Micro Transporter

If a figure carrying this device uses the Bait and Switch power, the target figure must make a Will (TN16) instead of (TN14) to resist.

Mindshackles

Once per game, if a figure carrying this device uses the Animal Control power, the Will Roll to resist the power is increased to (TN22) instead of (TN16). The choice to use this item may be made after the target figure makes their Will Roll.

Mindspike

Once per game, a figure activating the Suggestion power may choose to use this artefact. The Will Roll to resist this power is increased to (TN18) instead of (TN16). The choice to use this item may be made after the target figure makes their Will Roll.

Phase Manipulator

Once per game, if a figure carrying this device attempts to activate the Transport power they may choose to either gain +2 to the Activation Roll, or treat the power as if it were Strain: 0 (instead of Strain: 1). This decision may be made after the Activation Roll has been made.

Pickcaster

Once per game, if a figure carrying this device uses the Break Lock power, they receive +2 on their Activation Roll. This decision can be made after the Activation Roll is made.

Psychic Resonator

Once per game, if a figure carrying this device attempts to activate the Psychic Shield power they may choose to either gain +2 to the Activation Roll, or treat the power as if it were Strain: 1 (instead of Strain: 2). This decision may be made after the Activation Roll has been made.

Razor Derringer

Once per game, a figure carrying this device who has the Concealed Firearm power may choose to either gain +2 to the Activation Roll, or increase the attack generated to a +6 Shooting attack. This decision may be made after the Activation Roll has been made.

Reality Distorter

Once per game, a figure with the Cancel Power power carrying this device may attempt to activate that power as a free action.

Robolock

Once per game, if a figure carrying this device uses the Control Robot power, the Will Roll to resist the power is increased to (TN22) instead of (TN15) for the first roll only. Subsequent turns, the robot will make Will Roll (TN15) in order to end the control. The choice to use this item may be made after the target figure makes their Will Roll.

Sensory Tendrils

Once per game, if a figure carrying this device attempts to activate the Target Lock power they may choose to either gain +2 to the Activation Roll, or treat the power as if it were Strain: 0 (instead of Strain: 1). This decision may be made after the Activation Roll has been made.

SPENDING LOOT

After all of the players have determined all of the loot they accumulated in a game, they may now spend it!

NEW SOLDIERS

Players may hire new soldiers for the price listed on the **Soldier Tables** in Assembling a Crew (see pages 24 and 25). They may hire as many soldiers as they can afford, up to their maximum warband size, but are still limited to 4 specialists. Players are also free to remove soldiers from their crew. In this case, simply delete the soldier from the Crew Sheet. The player may take back any non-standard gear that the soldier was carrying, but otherwise receives no compensation or reimbursement. A player may also remove their first mate from their crew should they so desire, although this is likely to occur only if the first mate is suffering from multiple, debilitating, permanent injuries.

NEW CAPTAIN

Even the best sometimes fall in the firefights that fill the life of the independent crews. While this is a grim moment, and a huge set-back for a crew, it is not necessarily the end.

   If a crew loses their captain, the player has a choice: they can either scrap their entire crew and start over, or they can promote their first mate to be the new captain. However, they may only promote a first mate who is at least level 10. If they choose to promote the first mate, the first mate gets a special, one-time-only level boost. The first mate immediately gains 5 levels, and should select improvements based on the **Improvement Type per Level Table** (see page 75). The warband will need to recruit a new first mate as detailed below. There is no cost for hiring a new captain.

NEW FIRST MATE

If a crew loses its first mate, whether because it was killed, promoted to captain, or removed, they should immediately recruit a new one. Newly recruited first mates are created in the same way as detailed in Chapter One: Assembling a Crew (see page 22), except that they are immediately given a number of levels equal to their Captain's level -20, to a minimum of 0. The first mate should select improvements for each of those levels using the **Improvement Type per Level Table** (see page 75). There is no cost for hiring a first mate.

SELLING ITEMS

After any game, a crew can sell any Trade Goods, Secrets, or Information they have for the value listed for that item. They can also sell any Advanced Weapons, Advanced Technology, or Alien Artefacts for the amount listed in the 'Sell' column next to it.

BUYING ITEMS

If a crew desires, after any game it can see what rare items might be for sale. Each crew is allowed to make one roll on each of the following four tables: **Advanced Weapons Table**, **Advanced Technology Table I**, **Advanced Technology Table II**, and the **Alien Artefact Table** (see pages 80, 81, 82, and 91). The results of these four rolls are the only gear available to buy at that time. If a crew wishes to purchase one of the rolled items, they may do so simply by paying the amount listed in the 'Cost' column on the table.

IMPROVING THE SHIP

Every independent crew has a ship capable of intersystem travel – having a ship is what makes them 'crews' after all. These ships don't play a direct role in games of *Stargrave*; however, they remain a vitally important resource, and captains that find themselves with a bit of extra cash often like to invest in specific upgrades for the ship.

A captain can upgrade their ship simply by paying the cost listed below. A ship may never take a specific upgrade more than once, unless noted, but otherwise there is no limit to how many upgrades a ship can have.

SHIP UPGRADE TABLE

SHIP UPGRADE	COST	EFFECT
Advanced Medical Suite	500cr	This upgrade may only be used by a crew that contains a medic. The player may re-roll the Survival Roll for one soldier (specialist or standard) after each game. The second roll must be taken.
Armament Workshop	500cr	If a figure in the crew successfully uses the Armoury power before a game, the crew can field two suits of combat armour without having to pay their normal upkeep cost. Alternatively, two pistols, carbines, or shotguns may be given a +1 Damage modifier for the next game only. Or a crew may take one of each option.
Communications Array	300cr	Grants +2 to the Activation Roll for the Bribe power for any one member of the crew.
External Cargo Pods	300cr	The ship has extra room for carrying trade goods. Anytime this crew sells trade goods, it gets an extra 20% on top of the listed value.
Extra Quarters	1,000cr	A ship with extra quarters allows the crew to include one more specialist crewman than is normally allowed – 5 instead of the normal 4. The crew is still limited to 8 crewmen in total, however.
Meditation Chamber	400cr	Grants +2 to the Activation Roll for the Mystic Trance power for any one member of the crew. This upgrade may be purchased twice, and thus used by two different figures.
Robotics Workshop	650cr	Grants +1 to the Activation Roll for Create Robot, Remote Guidance, or Re-wire Robot for any one member of the crew when used Out of Game. This bonus may only be applied to one roll between each game.
Weapon Locker	600cr	Before each game, one soldier may be given a pistol, carbine, or shotgun that does +1 Damage that they may use for the following game only. This weapon is not indestructible, and takes up the soldier's gear slot.

OPTIONAL RULE – BALANCING SCENARIOS

As a *Stargrave* campaign progresses, it is likely that some crews will be more successful than others. They will gain more experience, and thus levels, and accumulate more loot. This will, of course, give them an advantage when playing against crews that have not done so well. In truth, unless the differences are large, this advantage is relatively minor, and less important than good tactical play with clever use of powers and lucky dice. Also, multiplayer games tend to be inherently balancing with weaker crews often ganging up on the stronger ones.

If players feel that their campaign has reached a point where some crews have a definite advantage, they might consider using the following optional rules at the start of a game. This table is designed for two-player games.

Start by determining the difference in level between the two crews. To do this, simply add the levels of the captain and the first mate together for each crew, and subtract the lower from the higher. If the difference is 8 levels or less, play the scenario as written. If the difference is 9 levels or more, consult the table below.

LEVEL DIFFERENCE RE-ROLL TABLE	
LEVEL DIFFERENCE	RE-ROLLS
9–12	1
12–16	2
17+	3

The player with the lower-level crew is given a number of rerolls. The player should probably keep a token for each of these close at hand to remember they have them. A player may spend one of these tokens to re-roll: a Fight Roll when rolling in defence against a Shooting attack, a roll to activate a power, or any Stat Roll with a Target Number. These are the only rolls that may be re-rolled under these rules. A player may never reroll the same roll more than once; otherwise, there is no limited to how many rerolls may be used in a turn.

CHAPTER FOUR
POWERS

All captains and first mates have special abilities that they can use to help their crew. In some cases these are mystic or psychic abilities, in others they are skills or tricks that have been learned through long experience. Players are free to imagine how their captains and first mates obtained their abilities and how they manifest them. Regardless of their exact nature, all of these abilities are referred to as **Powers**. There are over 50 different powers available, and it will take players a while to come to grips with them all. Some are very straightforward and enhance the stats of figures or allow the activator to make a special attack. Others, however, are much more subtle and can be used in a variety of ways to influence the outcome of the game.

POWER DESCRIPTIONS

Each power is fully described below, and all are presented in the same way as seen by this example:

Name

Activation: X / Strain: X / Category
Description.

NAME

The name of the power in game-terms. Specific captains and first mates may refer to their abilities in different ways.

ACTIVATION

This is the base activation number of the power. This number increases if the power comes from outside a figure's background or if it is taken by a first mate, as explained in Chapter One: Assembling a Crew (see page 12). The figure using a power is sometimes referred to as the 'activator'.

STRAIN

This is the amount of Damage taken by the activator if the power is successfully activated.

CATEGORY

The category determines when and how the power may be used. A few powers have multiple categories, in which case the player may choose which category to apply to a given situation.

Line of Sight

Powers of this type can be used on any target that is within line of sight of the activator. This includes the figure activating the power. Unless otherwise stated, the maximum range for line of sight powers is 24".

Out of Game (A or B)

These powers cannot be used during a game of *Stargrave*. Instead, they are used either before (B) the game has started or after (A) a game has been played. A figure that has one of these powers may make one attempt to use it at the appropriate time. A figure may not Exert when using these powers.

Self Only

These powers only affect the figure that activated them.

Touch

The activator must be within 1" and line of sight of the target. A figure may activate these powers on themselves.

DESCRIPTION

A precise description of what the power does.

ARMOUR INTERFERENCE

Some powers have (Armour Interference) listed at the end of their description. A figure attempting to activate one of these powers suffers a penalty to their Activation Roll equal to the Armour Bonus provided by their armour. So a figure wearing light armour would suffer a -1 to all Activation Rolls on powers with Armour Interference. A figure wearing combat armour would suffer -4. This penalty only applies to worn armour, not other bonuses to Armour given by powers or other advanced technology.

POWERS

Adrenaline Surge

Activation: 12 / Strain: 2 / Self Only
This figure immediately gains an additional action during this activation, and an additional action in their next activation as well.

Antigravity Projection

Activation: 10 / Strain: 0 / Line of Sight
The target figure gains the Levitate attribute (page 156) for the rest of the game.

Armour Plates

Activation: 10 / Strain: 2 / Self Only or Out of Game (B)
The figure gains +2 Armour. This power may not be used if the figure is already wearing combat armour. This power can be used Out of Game (B), in which case the activating figure starts the game at -2 Damage to represent the Strain.

Armoury

Activation: 10 / Strain: 0 / Out of Game (B)
The crew can field one suit of combat armour without having to pay is normal upkeep cost. Alternatively, one standard (not Advanced Technology) pistol, carbine, or shotgun may be given a +1 Damage modifier for the next game only.

Bait and Switch

Activation: 12 / Strain: 2 / Line of Sight
This power may only be used against a soldier carrying a loot token. That figure must make an immediate Will Roll (TN14). If failed, the figure immediately drops the loot token and the activator may move it up to 4" in any direction.

Break Lock

Activation: 12 / Strain: 1 / Line of Sight
Immediately unlocks one physical-loot counter.

Bribe

Activation: 14 / Strain: 0 / Out of Game (B)
If successful, place one bribe token next to the table and make your opponent aware of it. At any point of the game, when your opponent declares that a soldier (not a captain or first mate) is making a Shooting attack, but before the dice are rolled, you may play your bribe token. The Shooting attack automatically misses, and no dice are rolled. No crew may use more than one bribe token in any game.

Camouflage

Activation: 10 / Strain: 2 / Self Only
No figure may draw line of sight to this figure if it is more than 12" away. In addition, it gains +2 Fight when rolling against Shooting attacks from pistol, carbine, shotgun, or rapid-fire attacks. This power is cancelled if the figure becomes stunned.

Cancel Power

Activation: 12 / Strain: 1 / Line of Sight
Immediately cancels all effects of one ongoing Line of Sight power. It has no effect on powers with other designations.

Command

Activation: 10 / Strain: 0 / Line of Sight
Select one member of the crew that is in line of sight. That figure now activates in the current player's phase this turn. This power may not be used on a figure that has already activated in this turn.

Concealed Firearm

Activation: 10 / Strain: 1 / Self Only
This power may only be used while a figure is in combat. The figure may make one +5 Shooting attack against any other figure in the combat. Do not randomize the target of the attack, even if there are multiple figures in the combat. If this attack damages the target, it is automatically pushed back 1" and stunned, even if the attack did less than 4 Damage.

Control Animal

Activation: 10 / Strain: 1 / Line of Sight
This power may only be used against uncontrolled animals. The target animal must make an immediate Will Roll (TN16) or become a temporary member of the same crew as the activator. Each figure with this power may only have one animal under control at any time. They may cancel this power at any time as a free action.

Control Robot

Activation: 10 / Strain: 1 / Line of Sight
Select one robot in line of sight. That robot must make an immediate Will Roll (TN15). If it succeeds, nothing happens. If it fails, it immediately joins the crew of activator as a temporary member. The controlled robot may make a new Will Roll (TN15) after each of its activations. If it succeeds this power is canceled and the robot immediately reverts to its previous allegiance. A figure with this power may only have one robot under control at any time. They may cancel this power at any time as a free action.

Coordinated Fire

Activation: 10 / Strain: 0 / Line of Sight
The target member of the crew receives +1 Shoot for the duration of the game. This may not take a figure above +5 Shoot. A figure may only benefit from one Coordinated Fire Power at a time.

Create Robot

Activation: 14 / Strain: 0 / Out of Game (A)
The player may immediately add one robot soldier to their crew for no cost. This soldier can be of any type except Armoured Trooper, but the crew is still subject to the normal limitation on soldiers and specialist soldiers.

Dark Energy

Activation: 10 / Strain: 1 / Line of Sight
The figure makes a +5 Shooting attack against any target within 12". This attack ignores any armour worn by a figure (so subtract a figure's armour modifier from their armour). Increase this attack to +7 against robots. If this attack targets a figure in combat, do not randomize the target, it can only hit the intended target. (Armour Interference).

Data Jump

Activation: 10 / Strain: 1 / Line of Sight
This power may only target a member of the same warband that is carrying a data-loot token. The player may immediately move the data-loot token carried by that figure to another member of the crew, provided both are in line of sight of the activator and within 8" of one another.

Data Knock

Activation: 12 / Strain: 1 / Line of Sight
Immediately unlocks one data-loot counter.

Data Skip

Activation: 12 / Strain: 2 / Line of Sight
This power targets an unlocked data-loot token or a figure carrying such a token that is within 12". If the token is not being carried, the activator may move the data-loot token 4" in any direction. If a figure is carrying the token, then that figure must make a Will Roll (TN16). If failed, the activator may move the data-loot token up to 4" in any direction. Either way, the token remains unlocked.

Destroy Weapon

Activation: 12 / Strain: 2 / Line of Sight
This power may be used against any figure within 12". The activator may choose one weapon carried by that figure to be destroyed, except indestructible weapons. This weapon is replaced for free after the game. (Armour Interference).

Drone

Activation: 10 / Strain: 1 / Touch
Place a drone next to the activator (see Chapter Six: Bestiary, page 144). This drone counts as a temporary member of the crew, and may activate and move as normal. For the rest of the game, the figure may draw line of sight from the drone, instead of the figure, when using a power. This includes using Touch powers. A figure may only have one active drone at a time.

Electromagnetic Pulse

Activation: 10 / Strain: 1 / Line of Sight

If targeted against a robot, that robot must make an immediate Will Roll (TN18). If it fails, it receives no actions the next time it activates. If targeted against a non-robot figure, all firearms carried by that figure immediately jam as though they had rolled a 1 on a Shooting attack. Additionally, the weapon suffers a -1 Damage modifier for the rest of the game. A weapon can be jammed in multiple turns through the use of this power, but the Damage modifier only applies the first time.

Energy Shield

Activation: 10 / Strain: 0 / Self Only

A small energy shield forms around the user. This shield absorbs the next 3 points of Damage from any Shooting attack that would injure the activator. Once 3 points of Damage have been absorbed, the power is cancelled.

Fling

Activation: 8 / Strain: 1 / Self Only or Touch

This power can be used in two ways. The activator may use it while standing within 1" of a member of their crew, in which case they may immediately move that crewmember 6" in any direction, including up. However, the figure that was moved is immediately stunned. Alternatively, it can be used while in combat against a specific enemy figure. The target figure must make an immediate Fight Roll (TN16). If it fails, the activator may move the target figure up to 6" in any horizontal direction. The figure takes no Damage (unless there is another reason it would, such as falling), but is stunned. This power may not be used on any figure that has the Large attribute.

Fortune

Activation: 12 / Strain: 0 / Self Only

Place a fortune token either next to the figure or on your crew sheet next to the figure's entry. At any point the player may discard this token to reroll a Combat Roll, Shooting Roll, or Stat Roll made by that figure. If used, the figure must take the result of the reroll, they cannot choose to take the original roll. No figure may have more than one fortune token at one time.

Haggle

Activation: 10 / Strain: 0 / Out of Game (A)

This power may be used whenever the crew sells anything. The crew receives 20% more than the usual selling price. This power may only be used on the sale of one item after each game.

Heal

Activation: 10 / Strain: 0 / Line of Sight
This power restores up to 5 points of lost Health to a target figure within 6". This power cannot take a figure above its starting Health. This power has no effect on robots. (Armour Interference).

Holographic Wall

Activation: 10 / Strain: 1 / Line of Sight
Creates a holographic wall 6" long and 3" high. No line of sight may be drawn through this wall. Figures may move through the wall as though it is not there. At the end of each turn, after the turn in which the wall is placed, roll a die. On a 1–4 the holograph fails, and the wall is removed.

Life Leach

Activation: 10 / Strain: 0 / Line of Sight
The target must make an immediately Will Roll (TN15). If failed the target loses 3 Health and the figure using the power regains 3 Health. This may not take a figure above its starting Health. This power cannot be used against robots. A figure may use this power on a member of their own crew, but if so, that figure is immediately removed from the crew sheet and counts as an uncontrolled figure for the rest of the game. (Armour Interference).

Lift

Activation: 10 / Strain: 0 / Line of Sight
Immediately move one member of the same crew that is in line of sight 6" in any direction, including vertically. If this leaves the figure hanging above the ground, it immediately drops to the ground, but takes no Damage. The figure that is moved cannot take any additional actions this turn, though may have taken actions previously this turn. This may not move a figure off the table. (Armour Interference).

Mystic Trance

Activation: 8 / Strain: 0 / Out of Game (B)
If successfully activated, the figure may attempt to use one of their other powers before the first Initiative Roll as if it was an Out of Game (B) power. No power that targets a point on the table or an enemy figure can be used with Mystic Trance.

Power Spike

Activation: 8 / Strain: 1 / Self Only

The next time this figure makes a Shooting attack with a carbine, pistol, or shotgun, the shot does +3 Damage. This is cumulative with other damage modifiers for the weapon. For example, the total modifier would +4 in the case of a shotgun (+3 from Power Spike and +1 from the Shotgun).

Psionic Fire

Activation: 10 / Strain: 1 / Self Only

The activator should place two flamethrower templates as thought the figure had just made a flamethrower attack. These templates may be touching, but may not overlap. Every figure touching a template immediately suffers a +3 flamethrower attack (see page 57). Figures only suffer one attack even if touching both templates. (Armour Interference).

Pull

Activation: 12 / Strain: 1 / Line of Sight

The target figure must make a Will Roll (TN16). If it fails, move that figure up to 6" in any horizontal direction. This may not move a figure over terrain more than 0.5" high. If this moves them off terrain that is above the ground, they fall and take Damage as normal. (Armour Interference).

Puppet Master

Activation: 12 / Strain: 2 / Touch
Choose one non-robot member of the crew that has been reduced to 0 Health during the game. That soldier returns to the table, adjacent to the figure activating this power. The soldier has 1 Health and counts as wounded. They are treated as a normal soldier in every other way. Any given soldier may only be returned to the table once each game through the use of Puppet Master. (Armour Interference).

Psychic Shield

Activation: 10 / Strain: 2 / Line of Sight
The target figure is surrounded by psychic energy. The next time it is hit with a Shooting attack that causes Damage of any amount, halve that Damage (rounding down), and then the power is cancelled. It this figure is ever in combat, this power is immediately cancelled. If the figure also has an active Energy Shield, deduct then 3 points of Damage for it first, then halve the remaining for the Psychic Shield. (Armour Interference).

Regenerate

Activation: 8 / Strain: 0 / Self Only
The activator regains up to 3 points of lost Health.

Remote Guidance

Activation: 10 / Strain: 0 / Out of Game (B) or Touch
This power may be used on any robot soldier. That robot can always activate in the same phase as the activator, even if it is not within 3". The player is still limited to a maximum of three soldiers activating in either the Captain or First Mate Phase. An activator may only use Remote Guidance on one robot at a time.

Remote Firing

Activation: 10 / Strain: 0 / Line of Sight
This power allows the user to select one robot in the same crew that is within line of sight. That robot makes an immediate +3 Shooting attack against any legal target within 12". This attack does not count as the robot's activation, nor does it cost the robot an action.

Repair Robot

Activation: 10 / Strain: 0 / Line of Sight
This power restores up to 5 points of lost Health to a target robot within 6". This power cannot take a figure above its starting Health.

Restructure Body

Activation: 10 / Strain: 0 / Self Only or Out of Game (B)
The activator gains one of the following traits of its choice: Amphibious, Burrowing, Expert Climber, Immune to Critical Hits, Immune to Toxins, or Never Wounded. It may only gain one of these traits at a time, but can change the attribute from one to another with an additional use of the power.

Quick-Step

Activation: 10 / Strain: 1 / Self Only
A figure may not make a Power Move when attempting to activate this power. The activator may immediately move 4" in any direction, including out of combat. No figure may force combat during this move. The activator may not end this move within 1" of an enemy figure nor exit the table using this move. This move does not suffer any movement penalties for terrain. If the figure fails its activation, it may make a normal Power Move.

Re-wire Robot

Activation: 14 / Strain: 0 / Out of Game (B)
Select one robot in the crew. The robot may be given one of the following enhancements: +1 Move, +1 Fight, +1 Armour; however, it suffers -1 Will. These modifications are permanent. No robot may be re-wired more than once.

Suggestion

Activation: 12 / Strain: 1 / Line of Sight
The target of this power must make an immediate Will Roll (TN16). If it fails, it drops any loot it is carrying, and the activator may move the figure up to 3" in any direction, provided this does not move the figure into combat or cause it any immediate Damage (i.e. falling more than 3"). (Armour Interference).

Target Designation

Activation: 8 / Strain: 0 / Line of Sight
For the rest of the battle, this figure receives -2 Fight whenever rolling against a Shooting attack.

Target Lock

Activation: 10 / Strain: 1 / Touch
The activator may make an immediate grenade or grenade launcher attack as a free action against any point in range; it does not have to be in line of sight. The attack automatically hits its intended point. If this power is used during a group activation, then the grenade or grenade launcher attack can be made by another member of the crew that is within 1" and was part of the group activation.

Temporary Upgrade

Activation: 12 / Strain: 0 / Self Only
The activator may select one of the following stat increases: +1 Move, +1 Fight, +1 Shoot, +3 Will, +1 Armour. These may not take the figure above Move (7), Fight (+6), Shoot (+6), Will (+8), or Armour (14). A figure may only have one upgrade activate a time, but they may use this power again to switch from one upgrade to another.

Toxic Claws

Activation: 10 / Strain: 1 / Self Only

The figure immediately grows a set of indestructible claws. These count as a hand weapon, do +2 Damage, and are toxic.

Toxic Secretion

Activation: 12 / Strain: 0 / Out of Game (B)

The activator may select up to two members of their crew, including itself. All attacks made by those figures, including Shooting attacks, count as toxic for the next game.

Transport

Activation: 10 / Strain: 1 / Line of Sight

May target one member of the same crew that is within Line of Sight and 12" from the activator. This figure can be moved up to 6" in any direction (maintaining line of sight). If the figure was carrying a loot token, the token is dropped and not moved with the figure.

Void Blade

Activation: 10 / Strain: 0 / Self Only

A figure must be carrying a hand weapon in order to use this power. This hand weapon becomes indestructible and does +2 Damage. In addition, the figure receives +3 Fight whenever they are rolling against a Shooting attack generated by a pistol, carbine, rapid-fire, or shotgun. This bonus does not stack with cover; the player should use whichever modifier is greater. If this figure ever becomes stunned, this power is immediately cancelled. A figure with an active void blade cannot use any weapon that takes up more than 1 gear slot.

Wall of Force

Activation: 12 / Strain: 1 / Self Only

Creates an impenetrable, transparent wall, up to 6" long and 3" high anywhere within line of sight of the activator. This wall cannot be climbed (though any point it is anchored on may be). Grenade and grenade launcher attacks may be made over the wall. Figures may make a Shooting action at the wall. In that case, roll a die, on a 19–20, the wall is immediately cancelled.

CHAPTER FIVE
SCENARIOS

The first time you play *Stargrave*, it is probably best to just play a standard game as described in the basic rules. However, once you've got a handle on the mechanics, most players will probably want to quickly move on to playing scenarios. Scenarios represent unique and interesting encounters in the Ravaged Galaxy, and bring a lot more narrative to the game. They also give players the chance to earn more experience, often at the risk of greater danger. Before playing a game, players should mutually decide if they want to play a scenario and, if so, which one. Alternatively, they can roll for a random scenario on the **Random Scenario Table**. If the players are involved in an ongoing campaign, these scenarios should be treated as unique and no player should play a scenario more than once, if it can be avoided.

While each scenario has a specific setting, such as a town, a jungle, a spaceport, etc., players shouldn't worry too much about the particulars. If you don't have the buildings to construct a town, just change the setting to the wilderness and replace the buildings with big rocks or groves of trees. In general, it is the relative position and accessibility of terrain pieces that matters, not their appearance. In the same way, a lot of the scenarios call for specific creatures from Chapter Six: Bestiary (see page 139). If you don't have a miniature to match, that's fine, just proxy it with the closest thing you've got (or take the opportunity to pick up a cool new mini that fits the bill!).

Finally, I hope players will see the scenarios listed here as just the beginning. Once you've got a handle on the game, it is very easy to create your own scenarios. In such a vast galaxy, this is your chance to use all of the terrain in your collection. You can create scenarios set in medieval villages, volcanic mountains, even underwater. If you take some of the special rules seen in these scenarios as a guide, you should have no problem coming up with special rules that suit any given setting or scenario idea. In this way, you can tailor your campaign to suit the story you want to tell. You can even have several scenarios set in and around the same place as a couple of independent crews have a protracted fight over some rich loot! If you come up with some great rules for a low-gravity moon, go ahead and play a few games there to get the most out of your work! Creating your own scenarios is just another great way to push your own creativity in *Stargrave*.

RANDOM SCENARIO TABLE

Die Roll	Scenario
1–2	The Botched Deal
3–4	Salvage Crew
5–6	Steam Vents of the Undercity
7–8	Data Vault
9–10	Skymine
11–12	The Broken Fence
13–14	Starport Raid!
15–16	The Derelict Warship
17–18	The Overgrown Factory
19–20	Fire Moon

THE BOTCHED DEAL

You put the ship down in some sheltered hills and proceeded to the town on foot. It is a run-down, dust-bowl kind of place, the home of criminals, low-lifes, and the desperate. The plan was simple – make the trade as quickly and quietly as possible and get out of there. Unfortunately, someone else must have been tipped off, because as soon as you came within sight of the dealers, all hell broke loose.

SET-UP

This scenario is set on the outskirts of a small town. One small building should be placed in the centre of the table. Six more should be placed around the centre one in a very rough circle. The rest of the table should be filled up with scatter terrain such as crates, run-down or wrecked vehicles, waste bins, etc.

Depending on the type of terrain you have, the loot token placed in the centre of the table should either be inside, or on top of, the central building. This should be a physical-loot token. The other loot tokens should be placed as normal. After loot tokens are placed, each player should place one ruffian (see page 149) adjacent to a loot token of their choice.

SPECIAL RULES

Any time a player rolls a 1–4 for their Initiative Roll, they may place one ruffian adjacent to any building. All ruffians follow the standard rules for uncontrolled creatures.

The Target Point for this scenario is the closest loot token, whether or not it is being carried.

LOOT AND EXPERIENCE

Players should roll for loot as normal after the scenario.

Crews gain experience as normal for this scenario.

SALVAGE CREW

The space battle ended quickly. The pirate fighters raked the small cargo ship from stern to bow and sent it tumbling down to the planet below. As the pirates moved off, you came out of the shadows of the small moon and descended quietly down after the stricken ship. The chance of anyone surviving the crash are almost zero, but the chance of interesting salvage is much higher.

SET-UP

This scenario is set in a swamp. Place a small, crashed spaceship, or at least a large piece of one, in the centre of the table. Several other pieces of wreckage should be scattered around. The rest of the table should be densely packed with boggy pools, stunted trees, and tangled growth.

Place the crews as normal. Do not place the loot token that would normally be in the centre of the table, but place the other loot tokens as normal.

SPECIAL RULES

The wrecked spaceship still has some one of its automatic defence systems working. At the end of each turn it makes a +3 Shooting attack against the nearest figure that is in line of sight of the wrecked ship. The crews can neutralize this defence system by making an attack (shooting or hand-to-hand) against any part of the ship. Treat the ship as having Fight +0, Armour 20, Health 1. If the ship is reduced to 0 Health, the defence system is destroyed and makes no further shooting attacks.

A figure in contact with the ship may attempt to unlock it as though it were a physical-loot token (all bonuses and special powers that apply to unlocking physical-loot tokens apply to this roll as well). If the figure succeeds, immediately place a loot token adjacent to the figure; roll randomly to see if it is a physical-loot or data-loot token. If it is physical, treat it is unlocked. If it is data, it is locked. Only one loot token can be recovered from the ship in this way.

After the first turn, whenever players roll for Initiative, if the player who rolls lowest rolls an odd number, then that player must place one ryakan (see page 149) on the table in a table corner of their choice.

LOOT AND EXPERIENCE

Roll for loot after the game as normal, though a player that secures the loot token recovered from the ship receives 50cr in addition to whatever is rolled for that token.

Experience is gained as normal with the following additions:

- +5 experience points for each ryakan killed by the crew.
- +25 experience points for the crew that successfully reveals the loot token in the ship.

STEAM VENTS OF THE UNDERCITY

The gang took your credits, but the weapons they delivered were useless junk. Perhaps they thought you would have left the planet by the time you realized, or maybe they thought you wouldn't risk going down into the undercity to pursue them. Either way, they were badly mistaken.

SET-UP

Place six steam vents (these should be about 1" square), so that they form a rough circle around the middle of the table, with each vent being about 6–8" away from the centre. The rest of the table should be a crowded, industrial wasteland, filled with random structures, broken machinery and other refuse.

Place crews on the table as normal. Place a physical-loot token in the exact centre of the table. The other loot tokens should be placed following the normal rules, except that each player must place at least one token inside the circle of steam vents.

Finally, place one sewer-dragon (see page 151) adjacent to the central loot token.

SPECIAL RULES

Before the first turn, select two steam vents at random, and place an 8" diameter cloud of steam over each of them. Figures may move through clouds of steam normally, but figures may not draw line of sight into, out of, or through a cloud.

At the start of each turn after the first, randomly select one steam vent, and place a new cloud over it. If a figure is within 1" of a steam vent when it releases a cloud, they suffer a +3 attack. If they are under or in contact with the cloud, but not within 1" of the vent when the steam is released, they suffer a +0 attack. If a steam vent already has a cloud over it, it can still be selected, and figures suffer attacks as normal, but the cloud otherwise stays the same.

At the end of each turn, roll a die for each cloud. On a 12+ the cloud dissipates and should be removed.

Any time a player rolls a 1 or 2 on their Initiative Roll and the sewer-dragon is on the table, the player who lost Initiative may immediately move the sewer-dragon up to 4". This can take the sewer-dragon out of combat, and no figure may force combat during this move. Otherwise the sewer-dragon follows the normal rules for uncontrolled creatures.

Players that want to add even more chaos to this scenario should consider using the Unwanted Attention rules from Chapter Six: Bestiary (see page 141), but treat all figures rolled on the table as ruffians, to represent the various gang members attacking.

There is no Target Point for this scenario.

LOOT AND EXPERIENCE

Loot should be rolled for after the scenario as normal.

Experience is gained as normal with the following additions:

- +5 experience points whenever a member of the crew suffers an attack due to steam (to a maximum of +20).
- +25 experience points if a member of the crew kills the sewer-dragon.

DATA VAULT

The rumours of a mostly intact data vault hidden below the surface of a remote moon have launched a race among the independent crews. It is a race you intend on winning!

SET-UP

This scenario requires 25 columns (paint pots or small building blocks work well for this). Arrange the columns in a square 5 x 5 grid, with the centre column placed in the exact centre of the table. Each column should be about 4" away from its neighbours. The grid should form a diamond shape in relation to the table, so that each of the four corners of the grid points towards the centre point of one of the table edges.

The areas outside of the grid should be filled with rubble, either rocks or industrial debris. Some small rocks or industrial rubble should be scattered throughout the grid.

Crews should be placed on the table as normal. One distinctive data-loot token should be placed on or adjacent to the central column; this is the central loot token for the scenario. Each player should then place two additional data-loot tokens following the normal rules, except that they must all be on (or adjacent to) a column. No physical-loot tokens are used during this scenario.

SPECIAL RULES

Any figure equipped with a deck that is adjacent to a column may spend an action to attempt to move the central data token. This follows the same rules as unlocking a data-loot token. If successful, the player may move the central loot token to any column adjacent to the token's current column. The central loot token can be moved this way regardless of whether or not it has been unlocked. Once the central loot token has been picked up, it may not be moved in this fashion anymore.

After turn one, whenever a player rolls an even number for their Initiative Roll (i.e. 2, 4, 6, 8, etc.) they must select one figure that is within 2" of a column. That figure suffers an immediate +0 shooting attack as one of the columns suffers a violent electrical short.

The Target Point for this scenario is the central column.

LOOT AND EXPERIENCE

Roll for loot after the game as normal.

Experience is gained as normal with the following additions:

- +20 experience points if the crew uses a deck to move the central loot token from one column to another during the scenario.

SKYMINE

Your heart sank as the ship broke through the clouds and you caught your first view of the skymine. At one time it must have been a wonder, a giant floating city, held aloft by a strange combination of ancient technology and 'hard air'. Now though… the whole city seems to list slightly to one side, and most of it appears rusted, battered, and broken. As you approach, you see a couple of bits break away from the bottom and slowly drift down into the clouds. According to your intel, only the top dozen levels of the mine are still in use; most of it, the actual air-mining facilities, were completely abandoned. If it weren't for the rumours of valuable tech contained in those abandoned levels, you wouldn't even risk landing on the station.

SET-UP

This scenario takes place on the lowest level of the mine, where the sides are open to the air, and there are several broken holes in the floor. Start by placing 5 irregular holes on the table. These should be roughly 3" in diameter (circles of paper work fine). The rest of the table should be crowded with broken machinery, bits of wall, and piles of rubble.

The edges of the table within 3" of a corner represent staircases. Instead of starting table edges, players have starting corners. If playing with 2 players, each player is assigned two adjacent corners, and may set up all of their figures within 3" of either corner. If playing with 3 or 4, each player has one corner and must set up all of their figures within 6" of their corner.

Place loot tokens as normal. The central token should be a physical-loot token.

SPECIAL RULES

Unlike most games, it is possible for a figure to be forced off the table in this scenario. Any time a figure moves into contact with the table edge or a hole, or is pushed back while already adjacent to either, it must immediately make a Move Roll (TN12). If the figure fails, it tumbles off the table into the clouds below. Thankfully, due to heavy air, such figures fall very slowly, and can be picked up after the game. These figures are out of the game, but do not have to roll for Survival. They return for the next game with no adverse effects. Figures that pass their Move Roll stop at the edge and do not fall. Figures that can fly never fall and pass their Move Rolls automatically.

A figure can exit the table via their starting staircase to secure loot. A figure cannot be pushed off a table edge within 3" of a corner.

Whenever players roll for Initiative after the first turn, any roll of 1–3 indicates a heavy gust of wind (reduce this to 1–2 if playing with more than 2 players). Use the die with the lowest roll to indicate the direction of the gust (the point over the number on the d20, see Random Direction page 58, for examples). Each player makes Move Rolls (TN12) for each of their figures. On a success, nothing happens. On a failure, move the figure 2" in the indicated direction. They will stop if they hit any terrain at least 1" high. Otherwise move them over any terrain. If they are moved to the edge of the table or a hole, they must roll for falling as explained above.

There is no Target Point in this scenario.

LOOT AND EXPERIENCE

Loot should be rolled for after the game as normal

Experience should be gained as normal with the following addition:

- +10 experience points for each member of the crew that involuntarily falls off the table via a table edge or a hole (to a maximum of +40).

THE BROKEN FENCE

It's a quiet, pastoral planet, out on the edge of nowhere, and you visit it from time-to-time because it is the home of one of your best contacts – a fence who asks no questions and pays top credits. This time, however, as you set down in a quiet valley, you received no reply to your transmissions; nothing but static. Grabbing your gear, you lead your crew cautiously over the hills, until you can look down on their house. At first, nothing seems amiss, other than the general quiet, but as you look closer, you notice a couple of holes in the perimeter fence. A moment later, you spot something reddish-brown moving quickly and close the ground. It flashes around a corner and disappears into the house before you got a good look.

As you are trying to decide what to do, one of your crew taps you on the shoulder and points. Another crew is moving down a hill from the opposite side of the valley. You make up your mind quickly. You've got to get in there and investigate. If your contact is alive, they may need help, if they're dead, there is probably some valuable loot down there.

SET-UP

Place a small house or other building in the exact centre of the table. A fence 2" high surrounds the house, creating a square about 16" a side. There should be two holes, only a couple of inches wide, in the fence. In a two-player game, these holes should be on the sides that face the table edges not used as the player's starting edges. In games featuring more than two players, place the holes in two different randomly determined sides. The area inside the fence should be mostly clear. The area outside the fence should be filled with rocks, trees, a couple of small out-buildings, and maybe a worn-down vehicle or two.

The central loot token should be placed inside the building if the terrain allows it. If not, place it on top of the building. Each player must place at least one of their two loot tokens within the perimeter of the fence. Otherwise follow the normal rules for placing loot.

Place one ferrox (see page 144) next to each corner of the house.

SPECIAL RULES

The fence around the house is electric, but damaged. At the end of each turn, roll on the **Broken Fence Event Table** to see if an electric charge pulses through the fence, or if any new uncontrolled creatures arrive.

Uncontrolled creatures inside the perimeter of the fence will never move outside of it. Never count figures outside of the fence when determining their actions. When determining the actions of uncontrolled creatures outside of the fence, only count crewmembers inside the fence if the uncontrolled creatures has line of site to a hole in the fence – it will move towards and through that hole to reach them.

The fence can be climbed following the normal rules. A figure standing adjacent to the fence may attempt to make a new 2" hole following the same rules as for unlocking a physical-loot token. A figure adjacent to, or inside, the house may attempt to deactivate the fence by following the same rules as for unlocking a data-loot token. If the fence is deactivated, treat all Fence Pulse results on the event table as no event.

The Target Point for this scenario is the nearest loot token.

Die Roll	Event
BROKEN FENCE EVENT TABLE	
1–2	Fence Pulse. All figures within 3" of the fence suffer a +2 attack.
3–4	Fence Pulse. All figures within 2" of the fence suffer a +1 attack.
5–6	Fence Pulse. All figures within 1" of the fence suffer a +0 attack.
7–8	Fence Pulse. All figures in contact with the fence suffer a +0 attack.
9–12	No result
13–14	Place a ferrox adjacent to a random point on the table edge.
15–16	Pace 2 ferrox adjacent to a random point on the table edge.
17–18	Pace a shengrylla (see page 151) adjacent to a random point on the table edge.
19–20	Pace a 2 shengrylla adjacent to two random points on the table edge.

LOOT AND EXPERIENCE

Roll for loot after the game as normal. Experience is gained as normal with the following additions:

- +5 experience points for each uncontrolled creature killed by the crew (to a maximum of +30).
- +20 experience points if a member of the crew deactivates the fence.

THE STARPORT RAID!

You have nearly concluded the deal when alarm klaxons sound all over the station. 'Raid!' shouts your contact, just before they turn and flee down a corridor. In an instant the busy, but peaceful, station turns into chaos. People run in every direction, some discarding everything they were carrying, others taking the opportunity to loot. Gathering your crew around you, you race for the hanger. The pirates have come…

SET-UP

The table should contain four small spaceships (about 4" by 6" will do, but any size is fine as long as they don't completely take up the table). These should be numbered 1–4. The rest of the table should be crowded with cargo, machine parts, small vehicles, etc. Before setting up any loot or crew, each player has the option to place one repairbot (see page 149) anywhere adjacent to a spaceship. After this, crewmembers and loot tokens should be placed as normal.

SPECIAL RULES

At the start of each turn after the first, the primary player for that turn rolls a die. If the result is a 1–4, then the spaceship that corresponds to that number fires up its lift engines (if it isn't gone already). All figures within 4" of that spaceship immediately suffer a +4 attack. Determine the Damage from this attack as normal; move the figure directly away from the spaceship a number of inches equal to the amount of the Damage. Then halve the Damage, rounding down, and apply that to the figure as actual Damage. For example, if the Damage roll was 9, the figure is moved 9" directly away from the spaceship and takes 4 points of Damage. The edge of the table, or any terrain over 1" high, stops this movement, otherwise, move the figure over any shorter terrain or other figures. At the end of the turn after the turn in which a ship fires its lift engines, remove it from the table.

If the number rolled at the beginning of the turn is 5+, add the current turn +2 to the roll (so +4 at the beginning of the of the second turn, +5 and the beginning of the third, etc.) and compare the result to the **Unwanted Attention Table** found in Chapter Six: Bestiary (see page 141). Place any figures dictated by the table following the rules in the Unwanted Attention section.

Figures may only exit the table by moving off the table edge opposite the one where their crew started. Any figure that exits the table in this manner is assumed to have made it to their ship and escaped.

LOOT AND EXPERIENCE

Loot should be rolled for after the scenario following the normal rules; however, any figure that was reduced to 0 Health during the scenario, but survived, has been rounded up by the pirates. The crew may pay a bribe of 40 credits to get this crewmember back; otherwise they are treated as killed for campaign purposes.

Experience is gained as normal for this scenario with the following additions:

· +5 experience points for each member of the crew that escapes by moving off the table.
· +5 experience points for each pirate (of any type) that is killed by the crew (to a maximum of +30).

THE DERELICT WARSHIP

What an incredible stroke of luck. The derelict warship fell out of warp-space just minutes before you were due to jump out of the system. It looks old, and was obviously badly mauled in a fight, but sensors indicate that there are still large portions of the ship with atmospheric integrity. There is no doubt that, in a matter of hours, every independent crew within three systems will be swarming over the hull, but you've got a head start – a chance to get in there, grab the best stuff, and be away before the competition arrives.

SET-UP

Players should choose starting table edges before the terrain is set up. Once that is done, place a heavy wall straight down the middle of the table, cutting the deployment areas of both players in half. This wall should have three doorways – one in the exact centre of the wall, and the other two each 8" on either side of the central doorway. All of these doorways are open at the start of the game.

The rest of the table should be crowded with small sections of broken wall, broken machinery, cargo containers, etc. Place the central loot token in the middle doorway. The other loot tokens should be placed following the normal rules except that each player must put one loot token on either side of the central wall. After the loot tokens are placed, each player has the option to place one repairbot (see page 149) on the table next to either of the loot tokens their opponent placed.

If playing this scenario with three or four players, place two walls on the table so that the table is divided into quarters. The centre doorway should open onto all four sections. Each of the two walls should contain two doorways so that each quarter is connected to the two adjacent quarters by both the central door and one other doorway. Otherwise, play the scenario as written.

SPECIAL RULES

Any figure that is standing adjacent to a doorway, with no figures actually in the doorway and no enemy figures within 1" of the doorway, may spend an action to close the door. This door remains closed until another figure adjacent to the doorway spends an action to open it. There are no limitations on the position of other figures when opening a door. There is no way to lock a door in this scenario. An uncontrolled creature that is adjacent to the doorway when activated will spend their first action to open the door if it is closed.

At the end of each turn, the primary player should roll on **The Derelict Warship Event Table** below. The players should immediately apply the results from the table. Figures may only exit the table off their crews' starting table edge.

The Target Point for this scenario is the central doorway.

THE DERELICT WARSHIP EVENT TABLE

DIE ROLL	EVENT
1–2	No Event.
3–4	For the rest of the scenario, roll for Unwanted Attention (see page 141) as well as rolling on this event table each turn.
5–8	Part of the ship suddenly decompresses before emergency shields plug the leak. Select one side of the wall, and a random table edge on that side of the wall. All figures on that side of the wall must make a Move Roll (TN18). If they fail, move them a number of inches equal to the amount by which they failed the roll straight towards the randomly selected table edge. They will move over any terrain 1" or shorter. Any larger terrain or the edge of the table will stop this movement.
9–12	The lights go off for a second, before emergency glow-lamps kick in. All line of sight is reduced to a maximum of 12". If this result is rolled again, the lights come back on to full power and the line of sight rules return to normal.
13–14	All of the doors suddenly slam shut. Any figure even partially in a doorway suffers a +2 attack. Doors can be opened again as normal. If a loot token is in a doorway when this happens move the token 1" to one side of the doorway or the other, determined randomly.
15–16	The player that currently has the fewest figures on the table may place a damaged repairbot (see page 149) anywhere on the table they wish, so long as it is at least 2" from any other figure. This repairbot has already suffered 4 points of Damage.
17–18	Localized explosion. Each player may pick one point on the table. Every figure within 2" of that point suffers a +0 attack.
19–20	Reactor Core meltdown. Starting with the next turn, start counting down the turns from 7. When the countdown reaches zero, the warship explodes and any figures remaining on the table are automatically reduced to 0 Health. If this result is rolled a second time, immediately reduce the countdown by 2.

LOOT AND EXPERIENCE

Any figure that recovers at least one loot token during this scenario may select one of those loot tokens and make two rolls for it; the player may select which roll to use for that loot token. Other loot tokens should be rolled for as normal.

Experience is gained as normal with the following addition:

- +5 experience points for each member of the crew that exits the table after turn 3. Increase this to +10 if a figure exits the table after the Reactor Core Meltdown has begun.

THE OVERGROWN FACTORY

This was once a giant industrial complex a century or more ago. Now the roofs of most of the buildings have collapsed, the pavement has cracked, and the lush vegetation of the surrounding jungle has crept in to reclaim large sections. If you listen carefully, you can almost hear the creeper vines slowly crushing the concrete into dust.

After a long march, you finally reach your goal: a vast, broken factory that once manufactured weapons for one of the great empires. Inside, plants and machinery mingle together to create a strange maze, where vines wrapped around chains dangle from the remains of the ceiling. Suddenly, there is a coughing, grinding noise, and sections of the factory suddenly spring into life!

SET-UP

This scenario takes place inside a ruined factory that has been partially reclaimed by jungle. The table should be a dense maze of broken walls, large machines, and plants. Crews and loot tokens should be placed following the standard rules. The loot token in the centre of the table should be a physical-loot token.

SPECIAL RULES

At the start of the Creature Phase during the first turn, place a warbot (see page 152) at the centre point of a random table edge that was not used as a starting edge. (In a four-player game, place it in a random table corner.) Although the warbot is somewhat battered and its armour corroded, it is still functioning at its normal levels of lethality.

At the end of each turn, each player must select one crew member (from any crew), then roll on the **Overgrown Factory Event Table** and apply the result to that that figure immediately. No figure may be selected two turns in a row.

Players can also use the Random Encounter rules found in Chapter Six: Bestiary (see page 140) if they want to bring even more chaos to this scenario.

The Target Point for this scenario is the centre of the table.

OVERGROWN FACTORY EVENT TABLE

Die Roll	Event
1–4	This figure has stepped on a conveyor belt. It must make an immediate Move Roll (TN18), or the player that selected it may move it up to 4" in any horizontal direction.
5–8	A chunk of the ceiling falls on the figure. Make a +0 attack against it.
9–12	A machine right next to the figure suddenly makes a horrendous noise. The chosen figure, and all others within 3", must make a Will Roll (TN15) or be stunned.
13–15	The figure finds a box containing a few grenades. For the rest of the scenario this figure counts as armed with smoke and fragmentation grenades, even if they couldn't usually carry them.
16–18	A large flower spits a cloud of toxic fog. The figure must make a Health Roll (TN22) or be poisoned (see page 60).
19–20	The figure finds an interesting bit of technology. If this figure makes it off the table, the crew receives Trade Goods (50cr).

LOOT AND EXPERIENCE

Any player that secures loot tokens in this scenario may trade one of them for a roll on the **Advanced Weapon Table** (see page 80), instead of the normal loot table. Otherwise, loot should be rolled for as normal.

Experience is gained as normal for this scenario with the following additions:

- +10 experience points if the crew causes 1 or more points of Damage to the warbot.
- +30 experience points if the crew kills the warbot.

FIRE MOON

Once upon a time, it seemed that every remote and inhospitable corner of the galaxy contained a scientific research station. Now, nearly all of those stations are abandoned, most of them lying in ruins due to the harshness of the surrounding environment. However, it is that remoteness and inaccessibility that makes them so interesting. These stations often contained cutting edge – read: very expensive – technology, and with most looters unable to reach them, any station is a potential treasure trove. Which is why you've come to this dark, uninhabited sector, and set down on a moon criss-crossed with burning rivers of lava.

SET-UP

Place two rivers of lava, about 2" wide, so that the form a wiggly 'X' across the table, with each end of the 'X' running off one of the table corners. The rest of the table should be filled with the ruins of a research station and large hunks of volcanic rock.

Crews and loot tokens should be placed on the table following the standard rules.

Each player should take two magmites (see page 146) and place them off the table adjacent to their deployment area.

SPECIAL RULES

Anytime a figure enters a river of lava, for any reason, it immediately suffers 5 points of Damage, and may make an immediate free move to the closest unoccupied spot outside of the lava. Every time a figure activates while standing in the lava river, they suffer 5 points of Damage and must make a Will Roll (TN18) or be reduced to a maximum of one action during their activation. Figures with Flying or Levitate can move above the lava and do not suffer any of these penalties.

Whenever a player makes an Initiative Roll and the result is evenly divisible by three (i.e. 3, 6, 9, 12, 15, 18), they must place one of their magmites on the table if they have one remaining. The magmite may be placed anywhere in, or adjacent to, a lava river, and more than 1" away from any crew member. Each player may place a maximum of two magmites during the game. The magmites suffer no Damage or other penalties for moving through lava. These magmites are uncontrolled creatures.

The atmosphere of the moon is extremely thick and filled with ash, which makes breathing and exertion difficult. Anytime a figure wants to make a second (or third) move during a single activation, they must first make a Will Roll (TN10). If they fail, they do not move and the action is lost. Figures that have a filter mask, or who do not need to breath, such as robots, may ignore this rule.

LOOT AND EXPERIENCE

Roll for loot as normal after the scenario.

Experience is gained as normal with the following additions:

- +10 experience points for each magmite killed by the crew.
- +20 experience points for each magmite not placed by the player during the game (of their initial two).

CHAPTER SIX
BESTIARY

The galaxy is full of all kinds of strange and deadly creatures. This chapter presents just a few of the more common ones that the independent crews are likely to encounter during their travels. It is not meant to be an exhaustive list, and players are encouraged to make up their own alien creatures. Since the galaxy is so vast, just about anything can be justified. So if you've got a miniature that you've always wanted to use, but never had an excuse to field, simply create a stat-line for it, using some of the examples given here, and work it into a scenario. At the end of this chapter is a complete list of all of the creature attributes, which explains their special rules, and which can also help in creating your own alien monsters.

Along with the list of creatures, this chapter also includes two optional rules for how to work some of those creatures into your games, especially when you are not playing a specific scenario.

RANDOM ENCOUNTERS

When independent crews end up fighting in wilderness locations, it often attracts the attention of the native fauna, especially predators. When using this rule, they should immediately roll for a random encounter whenever a crew unlocks a loot token. Simply roll a die: on 10+, a creature has wandered into the battlefield to see what is going on. Roll on the **Random Encounter Table** to see what kind of creature has appeared. If the entry has a number in parenthesis after it, that is the number of creatures that appear. Each creature should be placed adjacent to the table edge at a random point. The creature follows all of the rules for an uncontrolled creature (see page 64), treating the centre of the table as the Target Point.

This rule increases the randomness of games, but it also greatly increases the narrative potential, and is thus recommended! Players may or may not want to use it when playing specific scenarios, as these often already have a mechanism for uncontrolled creatures entering play. It really just depends on how much chaos you want on your table.

This rule doesn't make a lot of sense for games that are set in an urban environment. For those games, you probably want to use the Unwanted Attention rule given later (see page 141).

Alternatively, players might want to create their own Random Encounter Table based on the figures they have in their collection. That way, when your roll for an Encounter, you know you'll have the figure available, and it will give you a chance to get some of those figures onto the table! Once you get more comfortable with the game, and start crafting your own scenarios, you might want to create specific Random Encounter Tables for each scenario, just including the creatures that you think are likely to be in the same area as the crews.

RANDOM ENCOUNTER TABLE

DIE ROLL	CREATURE	DIE ROLL	CREATURE
1	Ryankan	11	Dedfurd
2	Ferrox	12	Gaunch
3	Bileworm	13	Porigota
4	Ruffian	14	Mindgripper
5	Shengrylla	15	Horat
6	Primitive	16	Tanglers (2)
7	Primitives (3)	17	Sentrabot
8	Magmite	18	Warp Hound
9	Bounty Hunter	19	Warbot
10	Tangler	20	Sewer-dragon

UNWANTED ATTENTION

The problem with gunfights breaking out in urban environments is that they tend to attract attention – the wrong kind of attention. This can take the form of the local law-enforcement, if any exists, but more often than not in the Ravaged Galaxy, it is the troops of one of the pirate fleets, come to crush any outsiders who dare to trespass on their turf. This rule simulates this unwanted attention by having an ever-increasing chance of pirate forces showing up the longer a scenario lasts. It is also a good method to encourage players to be quick about their business and escape with any loot as fast as possible!

When using this rule, the primary player should roll a die at the end of each turn, add the number of the turn to the roll, and compare the result to the table below. If the table indicates any figures, these should be placed at a randomly determined point along the table edge. If the table indicates multiple figures these should be placed together, unless it indicates multiple groups (indicted by a '/' separating the groups), in which case each group should be placed at a different random point on the table edge.

DIE ROLL	FIGURES
UNWANTED ATTENTION TABLE	
2–14	None
15	Ruffian
16	Ruffian
17	2 Ruffians
18	Pirate Trooper
19	Pirate Trooper
20	Bounty Hunter
21	2 Pirate Troopers
22	2 Pirate Troopers / 1 Ruffian
23	2 Pirate Troopers / 2 Ruffian
24	Pirate Shock Trooper
25	Pirate Shock Trooper / 1 Pirate Trooper
26	Pirate Shock Trooper / 2 Pirate Troopers
27	Pirate Shock Trooper / 2 Pirate Troopers
28+	Pirate Shock Trooper / Pirate Shock Trooper

RANDOM CREATURE ENTRY

When determining where a random creature enters the table, simply roll a d20. Since each facing of a d20 is a triangle, you can use it as an arrow. Simply look at the arrow above the number rolled, and place the creature at the location on the table edge that it points towards. The actual number rolled here is irrelevant.

CREATURE LIST

This list contains all of the creatures that appear in the scenarios in this book, plus a few more that are used for the Random Encounter Table, or just presented to give players some ideas for possible scenarios. Each entry gives a brief description of the creature, followed by its stat line. Note that all of the abilities listed in the notes are explained in their own list at the end of the chapter (see pages 154–159).

Bileworm

These mostly featureless worms can grow over twenty feet long and as thick as a grown-man's leg. Because these creatures are completely boneless, they can squeeze into the tightest crevices, and often crawl into the works of spaceships, seeking warmth. It's actually possible for these creatures to survive for years in a spaceship's structure, leeching a small amount of power out of the ship's systems. When threatened, these creatures spit a sticky, acidic, and toxic bile. This spit has a range of 8".

BILEWORM						
MOVE	FIGHT	SHOOT	ARMOUR	WILL	HEALTH	NOTES
4	+2	+2	10	+3	12	Animal, Burrowing, Immune to Critical Hits, Ranged Attack, Toxic

Bounty Hunter

With the vast wealth of the pirates, it is often easier to just place a bounty on an enemy's head than it is to deal with them directly. Thus, the galaxy is crawling with bounty hunters looking to make a quick credit at the expense of the independent crews.

BOUNTY-HUNTER						
MOVE	FIGHT	SHOOT	ARMOUR	WILL	HEALTH	NOTES
6	+3	+3	11	+2	14	Carbine, Heavy Armour, Hand Weapon, Counting Coup

Dedfurd

These amphibious creatures resemble extremely large, bloated frogs. In their natural swamp environments, they have bright, colourful patterns that help them blend in with the algae. As their blubbery tissue contains strong anti-toxins, these creatures are often hunted for profit and they have been relocated to numerous planets across the galaxy. While these creatures spend the majority of their time sitting quietly and waiting for prey, they ferociously defend themselves if any threat comes close. When this happens, they spit a highly toxic mucus, then finish off the incapacitated target with their strong jaws. The range of the spit attack is 8".

DEDFURD						
MOVE	FIGHT	SHOOT	ARMOUR	WILL	HEALTH	NOTES
4	+2	+4	12	+2	16	Animal, Amphibious, Bounty (20cr) , Ranged Attack, Toxic, Large

Drone

These small, flying robots used to be extremely common and were used for all kinds of scouting and reconnaissance purposes; however, the anti-gravity technology used to keep them in the air has mostly been lost and is extremely expensive to repair. Thus, they are now generally only seen accompanying tinkerers and other robotics experts.

DRONE						
MOVE	FIGHT	SHOOT	ARMOUR	WILL	HEALTH	NOTES
6	+0	+0	10	+2	8	Fly, Pistol

Ferrox

This animal looks like an extra-mean combination of a wolf and fox. Unfortunately for farmers, they possesses the size and appetite of the wolf with the cunning and stealth of a fox. It is not clear how these animals have spread, but somehow they always seem to appear on planets that feature large herds of gentle livestock. While these predators generally favour easy prey, they will attack man-sized creatures if hungry.

FERROX						
MOVE	FIGHT	SHOOT	ARMOUR	WILL	HEALTH	NOTES
8	+2	+0	8	+4	12	Animal, Pack Hunters

Gaunch

The Gaunch are a race of human-sized scavengers, with giant bulging eyes, that hide in the shadows seeking out the remains from the carnage of the Last War. They generally wear little-to-no clothing, as the pigments in their silky skin are constantly changing to match their environment, making them nearly impossible to spot at any kind of distance. While they prefer to scavenge the remains of those fallen in battle, they will come out of hiding for fresh meat when the opportunity presents itself.

GAUNCH

Move	Fight	Shoot	Armour	Will	Health	Notes
6	+2	+0	8	+2	10	Chameleon

Horat

Horats are gigantic woolly rhinoceroses. At some point in the past they were apparently spread around the galaxy to use as pack beasts, especially in harsh climates. However, with the crash of civilization many escaped captivity, bred in the wild, and became feral. These creatures can be extremely aggressive, especially if startled or protecting young. They especially dislike gunfire of all types and attempt to quickly crush anyone who is firing.

HORAT

Move	Fight	Shoot	Armour	Will	Health	Notes
6	+4	+0	14	+1	14	Animal, Hatred of Gunfire, Horns, Large, Strong

Magmite

This family of highly diverse crustaceans live in the most extreme of volcanic environments. While they are poorly understood, they seem to derive most of their necessary energy from heat. That said, they do need to ingest organic matter in order to grow, and thus will usually attack any other living creature on sight. Standing about three feet tall, with a varied number of legs, claws, tails, and other appendages, magmites are covered in thick armoured plates that keep them completely protected from lava and most other sources of heat. Since these creatures are often encountered crawling out of fresh lava, they usually drip and spatter molten rock, which can be just as dangerous as their claws or mouths.

MAGMITE						
MOVE	FIGHT	SHOOT	ARMOUR	WILL	HEALTH	NOTES
5	+3	+0	13	+4	10	Animal, Lava Splash, Strong

Mindgripper

These parasitic monstrosities are only slightly bigger than a large rat and resemble a manta ray with little spider legs. When encountered, these creatures attempt to leap onto the back of their prey's head and pierce their skull with their barbed tongue. If this is accomplished, the creature is able to feed off the victim's brainwaves and actually control them for a limited time.

MINDGRIPPER						
MOVE	FIGHT	SHOOT	ARMOUR	WILL	HEALTH	NOTES
6	+2	+0	18	+3	1	Ensnare, Possess

Pirate Shock Trooper

Shock troopers are the elite soldiers of the pirate fleets. Only veterans who have been under fire multiple times can even apply to join the ranks of the shock troopers, and most of them don't make it through the vicious indoctrination program. Those that do are equipped with combat armour, organized into small fire-teams, and dispatched on the toughest, most critical missions. Few people stand and fight when shock troopers arrive.

PIRATE SHOCK TROOPER						
MOVE	FIGHT	SHOOT	ARMOUR	WILL	HEALTH	NOTES
6	+4	+4	13	+3	14	Carbine, Combat Armour

Pirate Trooper

The sad truth of the galaxy is that the pirate fleets now possess the biggest and best stockpile of arms and equipment. No one can match the strength of their armies. The vast majority of these armies is composed of troopers – well-armed and armoured soldiers with a basic level of training. While individually they are nothing special, when one shows up, you can bet that more will soon follow.

PIRATE TROOPER						
MOVE	FIGHT	SHOOT	ARMOUR	WILL	HEALTH	NOTES
5	+2	+2	11	+0	12	Carbine, Heavy Armour, Knife

Primitive

While starships move between solar systems, there are many groups that have never advanced much beyond the stone-age. These isolated groups are generally looked down upon by most of the galaxy, especially the rough folk who are most likely to encounter them in the current era. Thus, they are generally just called 'primitives', and ignored as much as possible. However, all too often, an independent crew will want or need something found in primitive land, and bloodshed often ensues.

PRIMITIVE						
MOVE	FIGHT	SHOOT	ARMOUR	WILL	HEALTH	NOTES
6	+1	+0	9	+0	10	Pack Hunter, Primitive Weapons

Porigota

Although they have a roughly humanoid form, these bulky creatures look more like giant insects, with a chitinous exoskeleton, giant bug eyes, antenna, mandibles, and heavy pincer-like claws. Amazingly, these creatures were purposely seeded on many planets, as they are popular targets for sport-hunters and their exoskeleton can be ground up and used as a high-protein food. While extremely dangerous, these creatures are generally solitary and not particularly intelligent, making them easy to lure into traps.

PORIGOTA						
MOVE	FIGHT	SHOOT	ARMOUR	WILL	HEALTH	NOTES
5	+4	+0	12	+0	14	Animal, Bounty (30cr), Large, Never Wounded, Strong

Repairbot

One of the most common forms of robot in the galaxy is the simple repairbot. While they come in many forms, they are all broadly similar – a simple robotic frame equipped with tools to handle specific jobs, which can be anything from gardening up to complex starship maintenance. Repairbots are not built to fight, but most can use their tools to achieve a measure of self-defence.

REPAIRBOT						
MOVE	FIGHT	SHOOT	ARMOUR	WILL	HEALTH	NOTES
5	+0	+0	8	+0	8	Robot, Unaggressive, Knife

Ruffian

In the rough parts of the galaxy where the Independent Crews tend to operate, almost everyone carries a gun. That doesn't necessary mean they have much skill with using it, however. Ruffian is a catch-all category that includes gang-members, low-level criminals, cheap bodyguards, and just about anyone who works in places where fights are likely to break out.

RUFFIAN						
MOVE	FIGHT	SHOOT	ARMOUR	WILL	HEALTH	NOTES
6	+2	+1	9	+0	10	Pistol

Ryakan

These large, leathery-winged creatures resemble a cross between a bat and a hairless bird with a four-foot wingspan. Vicious hunters, ryakans have no qualms about attacking man-sized, or even larger, creatures and taking a quick bite. While ryakans are air-breathers, and obviously need an atmosphere to fly, they have a habit of laying their small eggs in the nooks and crannies of spaceships. These eggs can survive almost indefinitely in a zero-gravity environment, only hatching when the outside conditions are right for survival. In this way, they have managed to spread all over the galaxy. Generally considered pests, many planets have a shoot-on-sight order for these creatures.

RYAKAN						
MOVE	FIGHT	SHOOT	ARMOUR	WILL	HEALTH	NOTES
8	+2	+0	10	+2	10	Animal, Flying

Sentrabot

One of the more common robot designs seen during the Last War, sentrabots featured extremely simplistic programming that essentially allowed them to serve one purpose: move along a pre-set path and shoot anything that got in the way. While most of these robots were destroyed in the fighting, a few are still found in more remote or deserted areas. Their masters may be long dead, but their programming remains and they continue to operate until disabled or destroyed.

SENTRABOT						
MOVE	FIGHT	SHOOT	ARMOUR	WILL	HEALTH	NOTES
5	+0	+2	12	+2	12	Robot, Immune to Robot Control, Surprise Shot

Sewer-dragon

Maybe it's the chemical cocktails found in industrial run-off, or maybe it's just biology, but wherever people have set up vast industrial complexes, or even vast habitation centres, various breeds of large, vicious lizards have been found lurking in the dark, wet corners underneath. While there is huge diversity in the breeds of these lizards, they are little studied, and nearly universally considered pests (incredibly dangerous pests, mind). Thankfully, most people can just avoid the areas they inhabit.

SEWER-DRAGON						
MOVE	FIGHT	SHOOT	ARMOUR	WILL	HEALTH	NOTES
5	+4	+0	12	+4	16	Animal, Amphibious, Immune to Toxin, Never Stunned, Strong

Shengrylla

Often called the 'Crazy Monkey', the shengrylla is a primate-like creature that stands about half the height of a typical humanoid. It is characterized by its three glowing eyes that exhibit a "crazed" look and a pair of prehensile tails. The Shengrylla use their extra sharp teeth to feed off the electrical energy stored in power cells and energy converters, and are thus often found near settlements. Shengrylla have a pair of prehensile tails which they can use to move quickly and gracefully over almost any terrain. While mostly seen as scavengers, the energy cells carried by the independent crews often attract the crazy monkeys and cause them to attack.

SHENGRYLLA						
MOVE	FIGHT	SHOOT	ARMOUR	WILL	HEALTH	NOTES
6	+2	+0	10	+3	12	Animal, Expert Climber, Sharp Teeth

Tangler

Standing about waist-high on an average human, these creatures resemble tough, leathery octopuses. Despite their ungainly movements, they are incredibly quick on their tentacle legs, expert climbers, and extremely hard to dislodge once they get their suckers on their prey.

TANGLER						
MOVE	FIGHT	SHOOT	ARMOUR	WILL	HEALTH	NOTES
6	+1	+0	12	+1	12	Animal, Expert Climber, Ensnare

Warbot

One of the most fearsome weapons of the Last War were the warbots. While they came in a nearly infinite number of forms, they were all large, heavily armoured, and brisling with weapons. They also featured multi-layer program-shielding to keep them from being controlled by the enemy. Very few of these military robots have survived to the present day, and there are no known production facilities still capable of constructing them. Still, a few are still operational, and where they appear, they are rightly feared.

MOVE	FIGHT	SHOOT	ARMOUR	WILL	HEALTH	NOTES
6	+4	+4	15	+6	20	Robot, Large, Immune to Control Robot, Multiple Shooting Attacks (3)

Warp Hound

Sometimes called 'The Spacer's Nightmare', these large, vicious, dog-like creatures are poorly understood, but thankfully extremely rare. Able to move through the folds in space in a way similar to ships, they can appear at any point at any time with no warning. Unlike ships, their ability to travel appears unaffected by gravity wells, and they are more than capable of 'jumping' straight onto a vessel, station, or surface of a planet.

Whenever a warp hound appears, its only goal seems to be to kill anything that gets close, especially anything that draws its attention by firing at it. It is unclear if anyone has ever killed a warp hound, for whenever these creatures suffer a significant wound, they vanish and do not reappear.

MOVE	FIGHT	SHOOT	ARMOUR	WILL	HEALTH	NOTES
8	+4	+0	13	+15	15	Hatred of Gunfire, Immune to Critical Hits, Immune to Toxin, Never Stunned, Never Wounded, Powerful

CREATURE ATTRIBUTES LIST

ANIMAL

A natural creature with less-than-human intelligence. Animals cannot interact with loot tokens and have no gear slots.

AMPHIBIOUS

This creature is perfectly happy on land or in the water. It automatically passes all swimming rolls, treats water as normal instead of rough ground, and suffers no Fight penalties for being in the water.

AQUATIC

This creature can only live in the water and will never willing move onto land. If forced onto land, it treats all ground as rough ground for the purposes of movement, and must make a Will Roll (TN16) every time it activates or suffer 5 points of Damage. Aquatic creatures never have to make swimming rolls, treat water as normal instead of rough ground, and suffer no Fight penalties for being in the water.

BOUNTY

There is some extra reward for killing this creature. The exact reward will be noted in the creature's description. This reward is automatically gained by a crew that kills it.

BURROWING

This creature can move through terrain as though it were not there, as long as it has enough movement to reach the other side (it cannot end its movement inside of terrain). Additionally, this creature never suffers any movement penalty for moving over rough ground.

CHAMELEON

This creature has some form of innate camouflage. No figure may draw line of sight to this figure if it is more than 12" away. In addition, it gains +3 Fight when making a Fight Roll against Shooting attacks from pistol, carbine, shotgun, or rapid-fire attacks.

COUNTING COUP

If this creature reduces a member of a crew to 0 Health through either a Shooting attack or combat, it has accomplished its goal. Remove this figure from the table.

ENSNARE

A figure in combat with this creature may only push the creature back or move away if it actually causes it Damage; simply winning a fight against this creature is not enough.

EXPERT CLIMBER

This creature suffers no movement penalty for climbing.

FLYING

The creature ignores all terrain and movement penalties when moving. Additionally, it never takes Damage from falling. Creatures with flying can move over the water without having to make Swimming Rolls; Swimming Rolls are only necessary if they dive into the water.

HATRED OF GUNFIRE

If there is a crewmember in line of sight that made a shooting attack this turn, the creature will ignore any closer crewmembers that did not make a shooting attack this turn when determining which models to target for move actions.

HORNS

If this creature moves into combat and makes a Fight Action as part of the same activation, it receives +2 Fight for that attack only.

IMMUNE TO CRITICAL HITS

This creature never suffers any extra Damage from a critical hit. Its opponent still automatically wins the fight on a roll of 20, but no additional Damage is inflicted.

IMMUNE TO (POWER)

This creature is immune to a specific power. That power has no effect on the creature and may never target it or do Damage to it.

IMMUNE TO TOXIN

This creature is never counted as poisoned (see page 60).

LARGE

This creature is very large and thus easier to target with shooting attacks. It suffers a -2 to its Combat Score when rolling against shooting attacks.

LAVA SPLASH

Whenever a figure in combat with this creature rolls a 5 or less (before modifiers) for their Fight Roll, they are splashed with lava and suffer an immediate 2 points of Damage.

LEVITATE

This creature never suffers any movement penalty for moving over rough ground or climbing.

MULTIPLE SHOOTING ATTACKS (X)

Whenever this creature makes a shooting attack, it may make (X) attacks using a single action. It will make the first shooting attack as normal. The second attack will be made against the second closest target in line of sight, the third against the third, etc. All shooting attacks after the first one receive a special -2 penalty. If there are fewer targets than the number of shooting attacks, it still only makes one shot per target.

NEVER STUNNED

This creature is never stunned, regardless of how much Damage it suffers from a shooting attack.

NEVER WOUNDED

This creature never suffers any penalties for being wounded.

PACK HUNTER

If more than one of these creatures appears at the same time, place them in base contact. Whenever a pack hunter is activated, all of the pack hunters in contact should be activated and moved as one. Roll randomly to see which creature is the 'head of the pack' and determine the pack's actions using that figure.

POSSESS

If this creature wins combat versus a member of a crew and causes Damage, it locks onto the crewmember and takes control of them. Treat the crew member as an uncontrolled character, and move the possessing creature with it wherever it goes. No figure may target the attached creature with a shooting attack (though they may target the crew member); they may only attack it in hand-to-hand combat. This creature and its victim do not count as supporting figures for one another. If the possessing creature is damaged, it loses its grip and may be pushed back. As soon as this happens, or the creature is killed, the figure that was possessed once again becomes a member of the crew as normal.

POWERFUL

This creature does x2 Damage.

PRIMITIVE WEAPONS

This creature uses weapons that belong to another era. They may be flinted tipped spears, bronze swords, or iron battle-axes, but regardless, they are not designed to cut through the highly advanced modern armours worn by adventurers. A creature armed with Primitive Weapons does -1 Damage.

RANGED ATTACK

This creature has some kind of natural ability that allows it to make ranged attacks.

ROBOT

This creature is never wounded. In addition it is subject to any rules that apply to robots.

SHARP TEETH

This creature does +1 Damage.

SURPRISE SHOT

This creature does not make shooting attacks during its own activation. Instead, it makes an immediate shooting attack whenever another model makes a move action within 12" and line of sight of it. This surprise shot interrupts the active figure's action, and occurs at the soonest point the figure is line of sight. If the active figure survives the attack, it may continue with its move and other actions as normal. This surprise shot can occur against any number of figures each turn, but the surprise shot will only be made against each specific figure once per turn.

STRONG

This creature does +2 Damage.

TOXIC

Any attack made by this creature is toxic. This creature is also immune to toxins.

UNAGGRESSIVE

If this creature is at its starting Health, the only action it will take each turn is one random move. It will never force combat, nor intentionally move into combat. If it does randomly move into another figure, move it away 1" and end its activation. If a figure attacks it, it will fight as normal. If the figure is ever reduced below its starting Health, it will follow the normal rules for uncontrolled creatures from that point onward. This attribute is immediately negated if the creature is controlled by any external source.

CREDITS

ARTWORK

Helge C. Balzer, Michele Giorgi, Sam Lamont, and Palao Puggioni

MINIATURES

Sculpted by Giorgio Bassani, Mark Copplestone, Bobby Jackson, and Bob Naismith.
Produced by North Star Military Figures.

PAINTING

Kev Dallimore and Dave Woodward

TERRAIN

Gale Force Nine

PHOTOGRAPHY

Wargames Illustrated and Kev Dallimore

SPECIAL THANKS

Brent Sinclair, Sasha Bilton, Jon Boker, Robert Stephenson, Gary Askham,
Volker Jacobson, John Stentz, Joshua Lowe, Dean Wilson, Søren 'Bloodbeard' Bay,
Landon Knoblock, and Maciek Mularski.

Official figures available from:

Nick Eyre's
NORTH STAR
Military Figures

www.northstarfigures.com

CREW NAME:		EXPERIENCE:
SHIP NAME:		CREDITS:

SHIP UPGRADES:

SHIP'S HOLD:

CAPTAIN:						LEVEL:
MOVE	FIGHT	SHOOT	ARMOUR	WILL	HEALTH	CURRENT HEALTH

POWERS

NAME	ACTIVATION	STRAIN	NAME	ACTIVATION	STRAIN

GEAR/NOTES:

FIRST MATE:						LEVEL:
MOVE	FIGHT	SHOOT	ARMOUR	WILL	HEALTH	CURRENT HEALTH

POWERS

NAME	ACTIVATION	STRAIN	NAME	ACTIVATION	STRAIN

GEAR/NOTES:

CREW:						TYPE:
MOVE	FIGHT	SHOOT	ARMOUR	WILL	HEALTH	CURRENT HEALTH

GEAR/NOTES:

CREW:						TYPE:
MOVE	FIGHT	SHOOT	ARMOUR	WILL	HEALTH	CURRENT HEALTH

GEAR/NOTES:

CREW:						TYPE:
MOVE	FIGHT	SHOOT	ARMOUR	WILL	HEALTH	CURRENT HEALTH

GEAR/NOTES:

CREW:						TYPE:
MOVE	FIGHT	SHOOT	ARMOUR	WILL	HEALTH	CURRENT HEALTH

GEAR/NOTES:

Adrenaline Surge

Activation: 12 / Strain: 2 / Self Only
This figure immediately gains an additional action during this activation, and an additional action in their next activation as well.

Antigravity Projection

Activation: 10 / Strain: 0 / Line of Sight
The target figure gains the Levitate attribute (page 156) for the rest of the game.

Armour Plates

Activation: 10 / Strain: 2 / Self Only or Out of Game (B)
The figure gains +2 Armour. This power may not be used if the figure is already wearing combat armour. This power can be used Out of Game (B), in which case the activating figure starts the game at -2 Damage to represent the Strain.

Armoury

Activation: 10 / Strain: 0 / Out of Game (B)
The crew can field one suit of combat armour without having to pay is normal upkeep cost. Alternatively, one standard (not Advanced Technology) pistol, carbine, or shotgun may be given a +1 Damage modifier for the next game only.

Bait and Switch

Activation: 12 / Strain: 2 / Line of Sight
This power may only be used against a soldier carrying a loot token. That figure must make an immediate Will Roll (TN14). If failed, the figure immediately drops the loot token and the activator may move it up to 4" in any direction.

Break Lock

Activation: 12 / Strain: 1 / Line of Sight
Immediately unlocks one physical-loot counter.

Bribe

Activation: 14 / Strain: 0 / Out of Game (B)
If successful, place one bribe token next to the table and make your opponent aware of it. At any point of the game, when your opponent declares that a soldier (not a captain or first mate) is making a Shooting attack, but before the dice are rolled, you may play your bribe token. The Shooting attack automatically misses, and no dice are rolled. No crew may use more than one bribe token in any game.

Camouflage

Activation: 10 / Strain: 2 / Self Only
No figure may draw line of sight to this figure if it is more than 12" away. In addition, it gains +2 Fight when rolling against Shooting attacks from pistol, carbine, shotgun, or rapid-fire attacks. This power is cancelled if the figure becomes stunned.

Cancel Power

Activation: 12 / Strain: 1 / Line of Sight
Immediately cancels all effects of one ongoing Line of Sight power. It has no effect on powers with other designations.

Command

Activation: 10 / Strain: 0 / Line of Sight
Select one member of the crew that is in line of sight. That figure now activates in the current player's phase this turn. This power may not be used on a figure that has already activated in this turn.

Concealed Firearm

Activation: 10 / Strain: 1 / Self Only
This power may only be used while a figure is in combat. The figure may make one +5 Shooting attack against any other figure in the combat. Do not randomize the target of the attack, even if there are multiple figures in the combat. If this attack damages the target, it is automatically pushed back 1" and stunned, even if the attack did less than 4 Damage.

Control Animal

Activation: 10 / Strain: 1 / Line of Sight
This power may only be used against uncontrolled animals. The target animal must make an immediate Will Roll (TN16) or become a temporary member of the same crew as the activator. Each figure with this power may only have one animal under control at any time. They may cancel this power at any time as a free action.

Control Robot

Activation: 10 / Strain: 1 / Line of Sight
Select one robot in line of sight. That robot must make an immediate Will Roll (TN15). If it succeeds, nothing happens. If it fails, it immediately joins the crew of activator as a temporary member. The controlled robot may make a new Will Roll (TN15) after each of its activations. If it succeeds this power is canceled and the robot immediately reverts to its previous allegiance. A figure with this power may only have one robot under control at any time. They may cancel this power at any time as a free action.

Coordinated Fire

Activation: 10 / Strain: 0 / Line of Sight
The target member of the crew receives +1 Shoot for the duration of the game. This may not take a figure above +5 Shoot. A figure may only benefit from one Coordinated Fire Power at a time.

Create Robot

Activation: 14 / Strain: 0 / Out of Game (A)
The player may immediately add one robot soldier to their crew for no cost. This soldier can be of any type except Armoured Trooper, but the crew is still subject to the normal limitation on soldiers and specialist soldiers.

Dark Energy

Activation: 10 / Strain: 1 / Line of Sight
The figure makes a +5 Shooting attack against any target within 12". This attack ignores any armour worn by a figure (so subtract a figure's armour modifier from their armour). Increase this attack to +7 against robots. If this attack targets a figure in combat, do not randomize the target, it can only hit the intended target. (Armour Interference).

Data Jump

Activation: 10 / Strain: 1 / Line of Sight
This power may only target a member of the same warband that is carrying a data-loot token. The player may immediately move the data-loot token carried by that figure to another member of the crew, provided both are in line of sight of the activator and within 8" of one another.

Data Knock

Activation: 12 / Strain: 1 / Line of Sight
Immediately unlocks one data-loot counter.

Data Skip

Activation: 12 / Strain: 2 / Line of Sight
This power targets an unlocked data-loot token or a figure carrying such a token that is within 12". If the token is not being carried, the activator may move the data-loot token 4" in any direction. If a figure is carrying the token, then that figure must make a Will Roll (TN16). If failed, the activator may move the data-loot token up to 4" in any direction. Either way, the token remains unlocked.

Destroy Weapon

Activation: 12 / Strain: 2 / Line of Sight
This power may be used against any figure within 12". The activator may choose one weapon carried by that figure to be destroyed, except indestructible weapons. This weapon is replaced for free after the game. (Armour Interference).

Drone

Activation: 10 / Strain: 1 / Touch
Place a drone next to the activator (see Chapter Six: Bestiary, page 144). This drone counts as a temporary member of the crew, and may activate and move as normal. For the rest of the game, the figure may draw line of sight from the drone, instead of the figure, when using a power. This includes using Touch powers. A figure may only have one active drone at a time.

Electromagnetic Pulse

Activation: 10 / Strain: 1 / Line of Sight
If targeted against a robot, that robot must make an immediate Will Roll (TN18). If it fails, it receives no actions the next time it activates. If targeted against a non-robot figure, all firearms carried by that figure immediately jam as though they had rolled a 1 on a Shooting attack. Additionally, the weapon suffers a -1 Damage modifier for the rest of the game. A weapon can be jammed in multiple turns through the use of this power, but the Damage modifier only applies the first time.

Energy Shield

Activation: 10 / Strain: 0 / Self Only
A small energy shield forms around the user. This shield absorbs the next 3 points of Damage from any Shooting attack that would injure the activator. Once 3 points of Damage have been absorbed, the power is cancelled.

Fling

Activation: 8 / Strain: 1 / Self Only or Touch
This power can be used in two ways. The activator may use it while standing within 1" of a member of their crew, in which case they may immediately move that crewmember 6" in any direction, including up. However, the figure that was moved is immediately stunned. Alternatively, it can be used while in combat against a specific enemy figure. The target figure must make an immediate Fight Roll (TN16). If it fails, the activator may move the target figure up to 6" in any horizontal direction. The figure takes no Damage (unless there is another reason it would, such as falling), but is stunned. This power may not be used on any figure that has the Large attribute.

Fortune

Activation: 12 / Strain: 0 / Self Only
Place a fortune token either next to the figure or on your crew sheet next to the figure's entry. At any point the player may discard this token to reroll a Combat Roll, Shooting Roll, or Stat Roll made by that figure. If used, the figure must take the result of the reroll, they cannot choose to take the original roll. No figure may have more than one fortune token at one time.

Haggle

Activation: 10 / Strain: 0 / Out of Game (A)
This power may be used whenever the crew sells anything. The crew receives 20% more than the usual selling price. This power may only be used on the sale of one item after each game.

Heal

Activation: 10 / Strain: 0 / Line of Sight
This power restores up to 5 points of lost Health to a target figure within 6". This power cannot take a figure above its starting Health. This power has no effect on robots. (Armour Interference).

Holographic Wall

Activation: 10 / Strain: 1 / Line of Sight
Creates a holographic wall 6" long and 3" high. No line of sight may be drawn through this wall. Figures may move through the wall as though it is not there. At the end of each turn, after the turn in which the wall is placed, roll a die. On a 1–4 the holograph fails, and the wall is removed.

Life Leach

Activation: 10 / Strain: 0 / Line of Sight
The target must make an immediately Will Roll (TN15). If failed the target loses 3 Health and the figure using the power regains 3 Health. This may not take a figure above its starting Health. This power cannot be used against robots. A figure may use this power on a member of their own crew, but if so, that figure is immediately removed from the crew sheet and counts as an uncontrolled figure for the rest of the game. (Armour Interference).

Lift

Activation: 10 / Strain: 0 / Line of Sight
Immediately move one member of the same crew that is in line of sight 6" in any direction, including vertically. If this leaves the figure hanging above the ground, it immediately drops to the ground, but takes no Damage. The figure that is moved cannot take any additional actions this turn, though may have taken actions previously this turn. This may not move a figure off the table. (Armour Interference).

Mystic Trance

Activation: 8 / Strain: 0 / Out of Game (B)
If successfully activated, the figure may attempt to use one of their other powers before the first Initiative Roll as if it was an Out of Game (B) power. No power that targets a point on the table or an enemy figure can be used with Mystic Trance.

Power Spike

Activation: 8 / Strain: 1 / Self Only
The next time this figure makes a Shooting attack with a carbine, pistol, or shotgun, the shot does +3 Damage. This is cumulative with other damage modifiers for the weapon. For example, the total modifier would +4 in the case of a shotgun (+3 from Power Spike and +1 from the Shotgun).

Psionic Fire

Activation: 10 / Strain: 1 / Self Only
The activator should place two flamethrower templates as thought the figure had just made a flamethrower attack. These templates may be touching, but may not overlap. Every figure touching a template immediately suffers a +3 flamethrower attack (see page 32). Figures only suffer one attack even if touching both templates. (Armour Interference).

Pull

Activation: 12 / Strain: 1 / Line of Sight
The target figure must make a Will Roll (TN16). If it fails, move that figure up to 6" in any horizontal direction. This may not move a figure over terrain more than 0.5" high. If this moves them off terrain that is above the ground, they fall and take Damage as normal. (Armour Interference).

Puppet Master

Activation: 12 / Strain: 2 / Touch
Choose one non-robot member of the crew that has been reduced to 0 Health during the game. That soldier returns to the table, adjacent to the figure activating this power. The soldier has 1 Health and counts as wounded. They are treated as a normal soldier in every other way. Any given soldier may only be returned to the table once each game through the use of Puppet Master. (Armour Interference).

Psychic Shield

Activation: 10 / Strain: 2 / Line of Sight
The target figure is surrounded by psychic energy. The next time it is hit with a Shooting attack that causes Damage of any amount, halve that Damage (rounding down), and then the power is cancelled. It this figure is ever in combat, this power is immediately cancelled. If the figure also has an active Energy Shield, deduct then 3 points of Damage for it first, then halve the remaining for the Psychic Shield. (Armour Interference).

Regenerate

Activation: 8 / Strain: 0 / Self Only
The activator regains up to 3 points of lost Health.

Remote Guidance

Activation: 10 / Strain: 0 / Out of Game (B) or Touch
This power may be used on any robot soldier. That robot can always activate in the same phase as the activator, even if it is not within 3". The player is still limited to a maximum of three soldiers activating in either the Captain or First Mate Phase. An activator may only use Remote Guidance on one robot at a time.

Remote Firing

Activation: 10 / Strain: 0 / Line of Sight
This power allows the user to select one robot in the same crew that is within line of sight. That robot makes an immediate +3 Shooting attack against any legal target within 12". This attack does not count as the robot's activation, nor does it cost the robot an action.

Repair Robot

Activation: 10 / Strain: 0 / Line of Sight
This power restores up to 5 points of lost Health to a target robot within 6". This power cannot take a figure above its starting Health.

Restructure Body

Activation: 10 / Strain: 0 / Self Only or Out of Game (B)

The activator gains one of the following traits of its choice: Amphibious, Burrowing, Expert Climber, Immune to Critical Hits, Immune to Toxins, or Never Wounded. It may only gain one of these traits at a time, but can change the attribute from one to another with an additional use of the power.

Quick-Step

Activation: 10 / Strain: 1 / Self Only

A figure may not make a Power Move when attempting to activate this power. The activator may immediately move 4" in any direction, including out of combat. No figure may force combat during this move. The activator may not end this move within 1" of an enemy figure nor exit the table using this move. This move does not suffer any movement penalties for terrain. If the figure fails its activation, it may make a normal Power Move.

Re-wire Robot

Activation: 14 / Strain: 0 / Out of Game (B)

Select one robot in the crew. The robot may be given one of the following enhancements: +1 Move, +1 Fight, +1 Armour; however, it suffers -1 Will. These modifications are permanent. No robot may be re-wired more than once.

Suggestion

Activation: 12 / Strain: 1 / Line of Sight

The target of this power must make an immediate Will Roll (TN16). If it fails, it drops any loot it is carrying, and the activator may move the figure up to 3" in any direction, provided this does not move the figure into combat or cause it any immediate Damage (i.e. falling more than 3"). (Armour Interference).

Target Lock

Activation: 10 / Strain: 1 / Touch

The activator may make an immediate grenade or grenade launcher attack as a free action against any point in range; it does not have to be in line of sight. The attack automatically hits its intended point. If this power is used during a group activation, then the grenade or grenade launcher attack can be made by another member of the crew that is within 1" and was part of the group activation.

Target Designation

Activation: 8 / Strain: 0 / Line of Sight

For the rest of the battle, this figure receives -2 Fight whenever rolling against a Shooting attack.

Temporary Upgrade

Activation: 12 / Strain: 0 / Self Only

The activator may select one of the following stat increases: +1 Move, +1 Fight, +1 Shoot, +3 Will, +1 Armour. These may not take the figure above Move (7), Fight (+6), Shoot (+6), Will (+8), or Armour (14). A figure may only have one upgrade activate a time, but they may use this power again to switch from one upgrade to another.

Toxic Claws

Activation: 10 / Strain: 1 / Self Only

The figure immediately grows a set of indestructible claws. These count as a hand weapon, do +2 Damage, and are toxic.

Toxic Secretion

Activation: 12 / Strain: 0 / Out of Game (B)
The activator may select up to two members of their crew, including itself. All attacks made by those figures, including Shooting attacks, count as toxic for the next game.

Transport

Activation: 10 / Strain: 1 / Line of Sight
May target one member of the same crew that is within Line of Sight and 12" from the activator. This figure can be moved up to 6" in any direction (maintaining line of sight). If the figure was carrying a loot token, the token is dropped and not moved with the figure.

Void Blade

Activation: 10 / Strain: 0 / Self Only
A figure must be carrying a hand weapon in order to use this power. This hand weapon becomes indestructible and does +2 Damage. In addition, the figure receives +3 Fight whenever they are rolling against a Shooting attack generated by a pistol, carbine, rapid-fire, or shotgun. This bonus does not stack with cover; the player should use whichever modifier is greater. If this figure ever becomes stunned, this power is immediately cancelled. A figure with an active void blade cannot use any weapon that takes up more than 1 gear slot.

Wall of Force

Activation: 12 / Strain: 1 / Self Only
Creates an impenetrable, transparent wall, up to 6" long and 3" high anywhere within line of sight of the activator. This wall cannot be climbed (though any point it is anchored on may be). Grenade and grenade launcher attacks may be made over the wall. Figures may make a Shooting action at the wall. In that case, roll a die, on a 19–20, the wall is immediately cancelled.

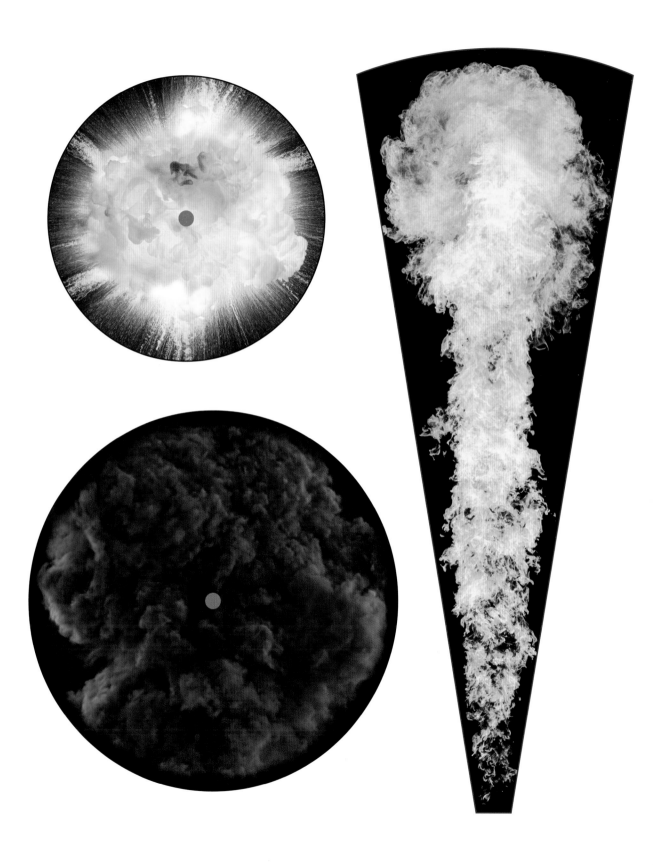

QUICK REFERENCE

TURN ORDER

- Initiative: Roll to see who goes first in each of the following phases.
- Captain Phase: Each player activates their captain plus up to 3 soldiers within 3" and LOS.
- First Mate Phase: Each player activates their first mate plus up to 3 soldiers within 3" and LOS.
- Soldier Phase: Each player activates all their soldiers that have not previously activated.
- Creature Phase: All non-controlled creatures activate.

ACTIVATION

All figures normally have 2 actions.

ACTIONS

- Move (must use one per activation).
- 2nd Move (1/2 distance).
- Fight.
- Shoot.
- Activate Power (including Power Move).
- Attempt to Unlock Loot.
- Special.

GROUP ACTIVATION

All figures in a group activation must move as their first action.

MOVEMENT

- Climbing or Rough Ground: 2" for every 1" or partial 1".
- Jumping: Figures can jump up to 4" horizontally, but must have moved the same distance in a straight line.
- Combat: A figure In Combat may not move.
- Forcing Combat: A figure not In Combat may intercept an enemy figure that moves within 1".
- Falling: Less than 3" – no effect. Greater than 3" – take damage = 1.5 x distance in inches rounded down.

- Swimming: Make a Will Roll (TN5), taking into account the modifiers (see page 47). If successful activates as normal. If it fails, no actions this turn and takes damage equal to the amount by which it failed its Swimming Roll.
- Run for it: For its first action a figure may move 3" regardless of any movement penalties. After having done so, their activation immediately ends.

COMBAT

- Both figures make a Combat Roll – roll a die and add the figure's Fight stat and any other relevant modifiers (e.g. bonuses from magic or supporting figures).
- Determine the winner by comparing Combat Rolls – highest wins.
- Add any damage modifiers to the winner's Combat Roll.
- Subtract the opponent's Armour stat from this total.
- Apply any damage multipliers
- If the final total is greater than 0, subtract that many points from the loser's Health. If it is 0 or negative, no damage is done.
- The winner now has the choice to remain in combat or push either themselves or their opponent back by 1".

GENERAL WEAPONS TABLE				
WEAPON	DAMAGE MODIFIER	MAXIMUM RANGE	GEAR SLOTS	NOTES
Flame Thrower	+2	Template	2	-1 Move. Target Armour and Cover modifiers.
Grenade – Fragmentation	-	6"	1	1.5" damage radius
Grenade – Smoke	-	6"	1	4" diameter smoke
Grenade Launcher	Grenade	16"	3	-1 Shoot
Hand Weapon	-	-	1	
Knife	- 1	-	1	
Pistol	-	10"	1	
Rapid Fire	+2*	24"	3	2 targets, -1 Move unless wearing heavy armour or combat armour
Carbine	-	24"	2	
Shotgun	+1	12"	2	
Unarmed	-2	-	-	-2 Fight
* Rapid Fire rules page 31				

MULTIPLE COMBATS

MULTIPLE COMBAT MODIFIER TABLE

CIRCUMSTANCE	MODIFIER	NOTES
Supporting Figure	+2	Every friendly figure also in combat with the target figure and not in combat with another figure gives a +2. This is cumulative, so three eligible supporting figures would grant a +6 modifier. Note that only one figure per combat may end up with a modifier from supporting figures, so if both figures are eligible for a +2 modifier they cancel each other out and both figures fight at +0. Similarly, if one is eligible for a +4 modifier and the other for a +2, the first fights at +2 and the second at +0. A figure may never claim more than +6 from supporting figures.

SHOOTING

- The shooter checks range and line of sight, then declares their target.
- The shooter makes a Shooting Roll – roll a die and add the figure's Shoot stat.
- The target makes a Combat Roll – roll a die and add its Fight stat and any relevant shooting defence modifiers.
- Determine the winner by comparing the shooter's Shooting Roll to the target's Combat Roll – highest wins.
- If the target is the winner, or the scores are equal, the attack misses.
- If the shooter is the winner, add any damage modifiers to the Shooting Roll.
- Subtract the opponent's Armour stat from this total.
- Apply any damage multipliers.
- If the final total is greater than 0, subtract that many points from the target's Health. If it is 0 or negative, no damage is done.
- If the target takes 4 points of damage, or more, they are stunned.
- Natural rolls of 20 are critical hits, while natural rolls of 1 are jams.

SHOOTING MODIFIER TABLE

CIRCUMSTANCE	MODIFIER	NOTES
Intervening Terrain	+1	Every piece of intervening terrain between the shooter and the target gives a +1. This is cumulative, so three pieces of intervening terrain would provide a +3 modifier. Note that if the target is in base contact with a terrain piece, it counts as cover instead of intervening terrain. If a shooter is in base contact with a terrain piece, it does not count as intervening terrain, though it may block line of sight.
Light Cover	+2	The target is in contact with solid cover (e.g. rocks, walls, thick wood, barricades, heavy machinery, other figures) that covers part of its body, or with soft cover (e.g. bushes, undergrowth, barbed wire, fences) that obscures half or more of its body.
Heavy Cover	+4	The target is in contact with solid cover that covers half or more of its body.
Hasty Shot	+1	The shooter previously moved during this activation

Large Target	-2	The target is particularly tall or unusually broad. This normally only applies to creatures who will have the 'Large' trait.
Stunned	+2	The target was stunned when it activated this turn.
Cleared Jam	+1	The shooting previously cleared a jam during this activation.

Throwing and Firing Grenades

- Select Target Point
- Make Shooting Stat Roll (TN12) apply modifiers Grenade Attack Modifiers Table.
- If the roll is failed, move the target point in a random direction a number of inches equal to the amount by which the roll failed, unless that number is over 6, in which case remove the target point.
- If smoke grenade, place a smoke template centred on target point.
- If fragmentation grenade, make a +3 shooting attack against every figure within a 1.5" radius.

GRENADE ATTACK MODIFIERS TABLE

SITUATION	MODIFIER TO SHOOT ROLL
Target Point is in Line of Sight	+2
Hasty Shot (The figure has already made a Move Action this activation)	-1
Firing with Grenade Launcher	-1

ACTIVATING A POWER

Roll a die. Roll must be equal to or greater than the Activation Number.

ACTIVATING A POWER ADDITIONAL RULES

EXERTION	Increase Casting Roll by 1 for every 1 Health spent.
STRAIN	If Activation is successful, the activator takes damage equal to the Strain of the power.
POWER MOVE	Activator may make a 3" move either before or after attempting the activation.

LOOT TOKENS

- Loot cannot be unlocked if an enemy is within 1".
- To Unlock a Loot Token a figure must spend an action and pass a Will Roll (TN14)
- The figure which unlocked a physical-loot token may pick it up as a free action. Any other figure may pick it up by spending an action.
- A figure must spend an action to pick up an unlocked data-loot token.
- A figure may only carry one loot token.
- A figure carrying a physical-loot token has its Move halved and suffers -1 Shoot and -1 Fight.
- There are no penalties for carrying a data-loot token.

CREATURE ACTIONS

Creatures will never attack another creature and will always force combat if possible.

1. Is the Creature in Combat?

Yes	No
It will use its action to fight. If it wins the combat, it will choose to stay in combat. If a creature is in combat with more than one opponent, it will attack the one with the lowest current Health.	Proceed to Step 2.

2. Is there a Warband Member in Line of Sight?

Yes	No
If the creature is armed with a missile weapon, and there is a crew member within range, it will shoot at the closest eligible target. It will take no second action. If the creature has no missile weapon, it will move as far as it can towards the closest visible figure, climbing obstacles as necessary. If it reaches a crewmember with its first action, it will use a Fight Action against them as its second.	Proceed to Step 3.

3. Random Movement

The creature will make its full Move in a random direction. If the creature moves into a wall or other obstacle, halt its movement at that point. Once this movement is complete, if the creature has an action remaining, check Step 2 once more – if no target has presented itself, the creature's activation ends, and no second action is taken, otherwise, proceed with Step 2 as normal.

POST-GAME SEQUENCE

After each scenario, each player should follow these steps in this order:

1. Check for injury or death (see page 68)
2. Use Out of Game (A) powers
3. Calculate experience and levels (see page 74)
4. Roll for loot (see page 77)
5. Spend loot